A Beautiful Stranger

A Beautiful Stranger

A Family Forever Series, Book 1

Donna Fasano

Find the author:

Facebook – Facebook.com/DonnaFasanoAuthor

Twitter – Twitter.com/DonnaFaz

Pinterest – Pinterest.com/DonnaFaz

Instagram – Instagram.com/Donna_Fasano

Contents

Introduction

Sean Hudson arrives to claim his new daughter only to discover the adoption hinges on the impossible. Unless he finds a wife immediately, the tiny orphan will be snatched away from him forever. But before Sean can abandon hope, a beautiful stranger proposes a surprising solution—a marriage of convenience.

Sean swears the love in his heart is only for his soon-to-be daughter. And that is perfect for Nicki Willis, whose restless spirit yearns to have a family for just a while. But the tenderness of Sean's touch soothes Nicki's fears as well as little Sona's. Soon Nicki aches to become a family forever... and she refuses to believe she can't make this dream come true.

Chapter One

"What do you mean, the rules have changed?"

Sean Hudson tried hard to keep his irritation at bay as he questioned the foreign government worker. The scarred and chipped battleship-gray desk between them seemed as formidable as a brick wall. And it wasn't the only barrier separating them. The man didn't understand a single word of English, Sean knew that. But his frustration was swiftly swelling into full-fledged, white-hot, scream-at-the-top-of-your-lungs anger. Wasn't anything going to go right here?

A dark cloud of dread descended on him as if in answer.

The man behind the desk—the person who held

in his hands the power to grant or withhold Sean's greatest wish—only shrugged. The guttural Slavic language he spoke had Sean automatically turning to the third man in the small room, the young translator he'd hired named Viktor.

Sean knew his impatience was showing.

"What is he saying, Viktor?" he asked, unable to quell the sharpness in his tone.

"He asks your forgiveness," the translator replied, his accent thick. "He says there is nothing he can do. His superiors have decided that you cannot take Sona from the orphanage. You cannot adopt her. You cannot take the child from the country."

Each *cannot* struck Sean like a boxer's swift jab to the jaw. The overwhelming disappointment wrenching in his gut was enough to make him want to double over in agony. How could this be happening? All the problems were supposed to have been ironed out *before* he'd left the United States. Now here he was, halfway around the world, finding out that his problems were only just beginning.

"I don't understand." Again Sean addressed the Kyrcznovian Child Services employee.

However, it was Viktor who explained further. "You have no wife, Mr. Hudson."

"But everyone already knew that weeks ago! I was told by the agency in the States—" Sean lost control, something he hated to do, but this stressful situation was enough to send him through the roof. He raised his voice and his speech became more animated with the use of his upraised hands. "My being single wasn't supposed to be a problem! I was told that the number of children made homeless by the war was rising at a rate that caused a flexibility of the law."

More conversation passed between Viktor and the government worker, and in that instant, Sean's eyes traveled down to the black-and-white photo he clutched in his fingers. He knew quite a bit about the toddler he'd come to Kyrcznovia to adopt.

The little girl depicted in the photograph looked so frail. Her dark brown gaze—"fearful doe-eyes" Sean had dubbed them—clearly depicted a vulnerability that had affected him to an astounding degree. Her nut-brown hair had been hacked off at chin length. From all reports, she was healthy—or rather, she *had been* healthy when he'd applied for the adoption eight weeks ago. Not knowing how she fared at this moment was torturous. He ran a gentle finger down the edge of the picture.

Sean wanted to be a daddy. No—he wanted to be *Sona's* daddy. Desperately.

The poor child had lost her parents when the couple had mistakenly walked across a small meadow just outside their border town that had been laced with land mines. *Kyrcznovian* land mines. Those two people couldn't have had a clue that they were taking their very lives into their hands, that their cutting across the field would leave their only child parentless.

This cute toddler—the child who had captured Sean's heart from the moment he'd laid eyes on her picture—had been orphaned by "friendly fire," as the U.S. armed forces would have called it. The very idea made Sean sick to his very soul.

Sona. His beautiful, lonely, *needy* little girl.

But these days in Kyrcznovia, Sona's story wasn't exceptional or unusual. So many children had been left hungry and homeless by the civil war raging in the small, newly developing country that the government had made a plea. People all over the world were called upon via the media to step up and help these kids, to come forward and provide homes. And families... and love.

Kyrcznovia was a beautiful land, filled with culture and wonderful people. And Sean was no stranger to the country. He'd visited here, years ago, when Kyrcznovia had been part of Russia, and his parents had brought him abroad. He'd stayed in this part of the country long enough to make friends. Of course, having been a happy-go-lucky twelve-year-old at the time, Sean had allowed himself to lose touch with the boys he'd met. But he never forgot the picturesque countryside.

At his home in Pennsylvania, Sean had been watching the evening news when he'd learned of the plight of the children of war-torn Kyrcznovia. Something deep inside him—something he still didn't quite understand—had been stirred, and he'd found himself calling the toll-free phone number on the television screen before he'd even realized it.

That had been two months ago.

Working through an adoption agency in the States, Sean had first procured Sona's name. Then he'd received her file and photo. Slowly but surely all the pieces had fallen into place. He'd even been told that his dyed-in-the-wool bachelor status was no problem. These children urgently needed to be placed in good homes. It mattered not that some of those homes would be headed by single parents. The agency back in America had *guaranteed* that his being single would not stand in the way of his adopting Sona.

However, now he was discovering that the assurance he'd been given was wrong. Resentment-stirringly, ire-provokingly *wrong*.

"That may have been so—"

The sound of Viktor's voice had Sean glancing up from the photo.

"—yesterday."

"*Yesterday?*" Sean didn't even try to hide his angry disbelief. "And will you please tell me what could have happened in the short span of twenty-four hours that has changed all the damned rules?"

Viktor smiled. "Forgive me, Mr. Hudson. That was just..." He paused. "How do I say it... a figure of speech. I did not mean *yesterday* literally."

When Sean didn't return the smile, the young man's humorous expression faded. "You see," Viktor continued, more seriously, "our country has just claimed its independence. Our government is just now being born. It is exciting. But there are... drawbacks. Our leaders are inexperienced. The rules here change from week to week." This time he couldn't stop his chuckle. "Sometimes from day-to-day."

Sean saw that his chances of taking little Sona home with him were dwindling by the moment. Tension bracketed his mouth as he unwittingly pressed his lips together tightly.

"We will get it right," Viktor promised. "Eventually. But you must try to understand. Everyone involved is only trying to do what is best. The—"

"What is best?" Sean raked his fingers through his hair. "This man—" he indicated the Child Services worker sitting at the desk "—honestly believes that it's best for me to go home *without* Sona?"

After a silent moment, Viktor softly said, "He is not trying to do what is best for you. Our government is trying to do what is best for the children."

"Those children are hungry!" Sean countered. "They're cold. They're scared. They're all alone in the world." Then he muttered in disgust, "Yet they're jammed into tiny, overcrowded rooms like... like little animals. There are twenty children for every adult caregiver in those orphanages. I've seen the reports. I know that—"

The man behind the desk spoke. And Viktor's response was so sharp, it had Sean asking, "What? What did he say?"

Viktor shook his head at Sean. "Nothing. He is only trying to lighten the mood. He made... how do I say it... a funny. No, a joke."

The sudden nervousness in the young translator's eyes caused the little hairs to raise on the back of Sean's neck. Something was up. Something wasn't right. "It didn't sound like a joke," he said.

Viktor only averted his eyes.

"I'm paying you to translate," Sean reminded the young man. There was a hint of warning in his tone as he said, "So translate."

"H-he said," Viktor stammered, "that for a hundred of your American dollars he would find you a young and sturdy Kyrcznovian wife. He said it would take him two days only. He suggests you go home with a whole new family."

At the sound of the word *wife*, Sean's chin dipped low and his whole body tensed. A permanent relationship was something he'd never have. Never.

"He meant no harm," Viktor rushed to say. "If you are not interested, he understands. However, if his superiors were to discover his offer, he would lose his job. Your discretion is much appreciated."

Sean took a moment to steel himself before looking directly into Viktor's face, his own eyes reflecting a harshness he was simply unable to contain.

"As you said," Sean replied, his jaw remaining tight and unyielding, "he was only making a joke." After giving the man behind the desk an unsmiling nod, he turned to leave.

"Mr. Hudson," Viktor called after him, "please remember that the rules could again change. Next month. Next week. Even tomorrow. Please do not be discouraged."

Discouraged didn't begin to describe how Sean felt. He'd come too far, both in physical miles and in emotional commitment, to leave this country without that little girl. But he was devastated to realize that he had so little say in the most important matter of Sona's life, in the most important matter of his *own* life.

Sean didn't bother responding to Viktor's encouragement. Instead he just kept walking down the dingy green hallway, his heart so heavy he felt as if it were a hunk of jagged lead wedged against his ribs.

***

Nicole Willis was in a fix. However, she wasn't too worried about the situation. Sure, this turn of events was unexpected. But she'd been in this position before. Well...maybe not this *particular* position, with no job, no money, and no prospects for either in anything resembling the near future. However, something would turn up. Some solution to her problem would soon present itself. It always did.

This hotel and its restaurant looked quite modern compared to the dozen or so others she'd visited this morning. She pushed her way through the door and scanned the room. Several customers sat at tables that had been meticulously lined into even rows. One dark-haired man, Nicki couldn't help noticing, sat staring into his coffee mug as if he had the weight of the whole world on his shoulders. The clean, white tablecloths had a crisp stiffness that only plenty of starch and a hot iron could achieve. The floor was spotless, and so were the fresh white shirts of the staff. She wouldn't mind working in a place like this. At least, until she could make enough money to travel to her next teaching assignment.

Nicki got the attention of a waiter and asked where she might find the man in charge. Without stopping on his trek toward the kitchen, the waiter pointed toward the back of the room. Her gaze followed his direction and she saw the door to what could only be the manager's office. With purposeful steps, she made a beeline for it.

She smoothed her palms down the fabric of her skirt, rehearsing in her head her most persuasive arguments. She urgently needed a job. For if she didn't make some money soon, she'd be in deep trouble.

Shaking her head, she shoved aside the cloud of worry and focused instead on what she would say that would procure her employment here. She simply had to find a paying position for herself. Today!

***

The coffee in the heavy ceramic mug Sean cradled between his palms was bitter and so strong that it had nearly burned away his taste buds since he'd been idling away his time here in the hotel's restaurant. The past four days since he'd walked out of the Child Services department had been the longest of his life. The hours seemed to draw out into endless infinity. And in all of that time little Sona had never left his mind.

Was she hungry? Hurting? Frightened? Was she being watched closely in that overcrowded orphanage? Or was she being teased? Tormented? Abused?

Every single moment of not knowing was sheer agony for him. Were these the kinds of worries parents suffered for their children? Were these the fears a father felt...?

Something akin to a tap on his shoulder had his chin lifting, although no one was close enough to touch him. His gaze was automatically drawn to the woman making her way toward the back of the restaurant

Her glorious head of long, wavy red hair was utterly striking. Her face was hidden from clear view, but he could see the rest of her...all five and a half feet of her feminine curves. He soon had a rear view, and the way her fanny gently swayed from side to side with each step was enough to make any red-blooded man salivate.

Sean swallowed, his gaze darting down to his

mug of coffee. Then he shot her another quick look, just in time to see her lift her balled-up hand and rap on the office door.

The woman participated in a fluid, unhesitating conversation with the elderly man Sean knew to be the restaurant manager. However, even though she spoke the language of Kyrcznovia, wore the same clothing as other women he'd seen on the streets and in the shops, there was still something ...*off*, something not quite right about the scene he watched unfolding. But he couldn't put his finger on what it was.

When her tone turned urgent, and then pleading, Sean became openly riveted to what was taking place between the man and woman at the far end of the room. He heard her say, "*Prosím,*" several times.

Now, Sean didn't know much Kyrcznovian, but during his daily visits to the Child Services building with Viktor, he'd discovered how to pronounce *please* perfectly...and he had. Many times.

The woman was obviously in some kind of trouble. She was either trying to explain her problem to the manager, or she was begging him to help her solve it. Sean couldn't say which.

He wondered what misfortune she...

Blinking, he caught himself and stopped the thought, midstream.

What was he doing? He shouldn't be wasting energy pondering someone else's dilemma. And some woman's at that!

He'd made a solemn vow to himself years ago that he'd make a berth around people of the female persuasion. A *wide* berth.

It was then that the manager firmly shut the office door—right in the woman's face. The defeat and weariness in her rounded shoulders had Sean up and out of his seat before he even realized it.

You will not speak to her, a stern voice told him. *You've got enough problems of your own. Walk right on by. The door to the rest room is just ten feet away. Head for it. Now!*

It was good advice. It really was. And he had every intention of following the silent commands the oh-so-logical part of his brain dictated. But just as he got near her, she heaved a heavy sigh and whispered, "Oh, my."

Sean stopped in his tracks so abruptly that he had to lift his arms just a fraction to keep his balance. "You speak English."

At the sound of his voice, she reached up,

tucked the silky tresses of her hair behind her ear and looked him full in the face. She gave him the barest hint of a smile, and Sean felt as if he'd been clobbered over the head with a thick length of two-by-four.

This woman wasn't merely beautiful, she was gorgeous. She was young. Maybe in her mid-twenties. Her wide-set eyes were the deep green of the rarest of emeralds, her tawny brows forming perfect arches hovering over them. Surely an exceptionally talented artist had delicately sculpted that tiny button nose and those high cheekbones.

Then his attention was totally captured by her lips...or rather, the flawless Cupid's bow of her upper lip. Hers was the most sensual, the most kissable mouth he'd ever seen in his entire life.

"You're..." The word came out in a husky whisper.

Stunning, he'd been about to say. But, thankfully, he was able to stop the utterance from rolling off his tongue.

He must be crazy! All this worrying and fretting over his predicament with Sona had surely made him take a tumble off the deep end into total insanity.

You can't go around tossing out compliments to complete strangers. In a foreign country, at that. What on earth are you thinking?

"An American?" she finished what she evidently thought he'd been about to say.

Her smile widened a fraction as if to let him know that she'd been approached plenty of times by people—just like him—who were surprised to find an American dressing, speaking, *living* as any other native of Kyrcznovia. But he wasn't like all those other people who had been taken off guard by her nationality. He hadn't been about to comment on those things at all. Instead, he had been about to make an absolute fool of himself, and he'd be lying through his teeth if he said he wasn't relieved that she had mistaken his unfinished thought.

She softly added, "Yes, I am."

"Ah," was his only response. Several different questions rolled through his mind at the same time. What was she doing in the chaos of a brand-new country? Didn't she know such political unrest carried danger for traveling foreigners? Where, in heaven's name, had she inherited those exquisite jewel-green eyes? Or rather, *from whom*, he guessed was the correct turn of phrase...

Something in him stirred. Something deep. Primal. At gut level.

He moistened his dry lips and tried to smile, but for some unfathomable reason he couldn't get his facial muscles to work. "You...ah, I..." he began. But words failed him. Being this tongue-tied confused him. After taking a quick, deep breath, he made another attempt. "I couldn't help overhearing your, ah, conversation," he confessed. Then a small chuckle escaped from his throat. "I don't speak the language, but... you seemed to be conveying that... you're in some sort of trouble."

The inflection he placed on his observance put an inquiring twist on his statement. He wanted her to confide in him. That was the last thing he *should* have wanted at this moment. The very last thing. However, Sean was simply too intrigued by the fiery-haired woman to listen to logic.

Nicki couldn't help the earnest smile that tugged and then lingered on her lips. This man—this stranger—was expressing concern for her. And she was touched.

But what moved her most was realizing that this was the very man whom she had noticed studying his coffee with such focused, contemplative intent when she'd first entered the restaurant. She vaguely remembered making an unwitting assessment even then that he was obviously someone with a load of worries on his mind. However, here he was inquiring about hers. The idea was soul-warming to say the least, and it told her something about the man. Something important. However, Nicki wouldn't dream of adding to his problems by unloading hers onto him, too.

"Thanks for your kindness, but there's nothing to worry about." She hoped her appreciative tone let him see exactly how she felt about his concern for her. Reaching out she touched him gently on the forearm—and was surprised speechless as a hot shock wave rolled across her skin.

She'd meant to assure him further that she'd be just fine. That her problem wasn't anything she couldn't handle. However, all she was cognizant of was the hardness of the corded muscles underneath the sleeve of his suit jacket. And the heat.

Her fingertips absorbed the warmth of his body and she felt suddenly feverish as the swelter fairly pulsed from him... and into her. Her skin flamed, from her neck and cheeks, all the way to the roots of her hair. It took every ounce of her strength to withdraw her hand from his arm.

"I—I'm," she stammered. Stopped. Swallowed. Then tried again. "I'm going to be fine."

But for the life of her she couldn't quite figure out if she was trying to reassure him—or herself.

Nicki was mortified by her involuntary reaction to this man. A complete and total stranger. Things like this didn't happen to her. Surely, he must think she was some kind of forward floozy who...

At that moment, the low growl of a hunger pang rumbled from her tummy, further embarrassing her. She automatically pressed her hand against her stomach and murmured a quick, "Pardon me."

The comers of his mouth curled, but there wasn't a hint of teasing in his deep mahogany eyes when he said softly, "I'd like to invite you to lunch, but—" he shrugged "—I don't even know your name."

His gaze seemed to hold her spellbound. "Nicole," she responded, her voice sounding very far away to her own ears. "Nicki Willis."

She found herself helplessly studying his ruggedly handsome face—the wide, sexy mouth that smiled so charmingly, his clean-shaven jaw, his perfect, bladelike nose, those deep-brown, intense eyes fanned with dark lashes and thick brows, and finally his high forehead, feathered with light worry lines. His hair was the color of strong, rich coffee; its satiny texture glistened in the afternoon light. One errant lock curled downward and she had to fight the urge to reach up and comb it back with her fingers. He was a startlingly handsome man.

Suddenly realizing that her breath had become shallow, and worse yet, that she was staring, she took a quick, deep breath, blinked twice, and averted her gaze.

Marvelous man that he was, he picked up the conversation as if the too obvious lag had never occurred.

"Well, Nicki," he said easily, "let me buy you lunch."

"Oh, no." She shook her head. "I couldn't impose—"

He cut her off. "Nonsense. It would only be an imposition if you were keeping me from something, or if I had to be somewhere." Then his face grew strained as he added, "The truth is, Nicki, you'd be offering me a respite..."

She studied him intently, sure he was about to

reveal some tidbit of information regarding what was troubling him. But he didn't.

"...if you were to let me buy you something to eat."

Nicki knew she shouldn't even consider his offer. He was a nice man. A nice, *handsome* man. A man who didn't need to listen to her woes. And besides that, she needed to find a job. Today. And she wouldn't find any success in dawdling here with this nice, handsome man.

Another low rumble resounded from her stomach, and they both smiled in unison.

"What do you say, Nicki?" he asked, his tone charming. Inviting. *Alluring.* "Will you have lunch with me? Will you tell me what's troubling you?"

She sighed. She was hungry. And letting him buy her a meal would be a solid financial decision on her part, wouldn't it?

"Only if you'll tell me your name," she said. "And... if you'll tell me what's troubling *you.*"

He told her his name was Sean Hudson, and the look of surprise that had invaded his features remained staunchly in place until they were seated at the table, menus in hand.

"So, how did you know?" he finally asked.

She grinned. "That you have problems of your

own?" One of her shoulders lifted a fraction. "Guess you could say I'm the observant type."

He nodded, seeming to accept the explanation. Then she decided to be completely honest "When I came through the door, I saw you studying your coffee mug like it contained some deep, enigmatic secret that you were bent on discovering."

Sean chuckled, and Nicki was sure it had to be one of the most pleasant sounds she'd ever heard. "I see," he told her.

The waiter took their orders, and then Sean asked, "So, what was that between you and the manager of this place?"

The sigh Nicki expelled sounded tired, even to her. "He was turning me down for a job. It's very hard for a female to find employment in Kyrcznovia."

He frowned. "Well, what are you doing in the country without employment? How do you survive?"

"Oh, I had a job." Then she grimaced. "*Had* being the operative word. You see, I was teaching several groups of children English. The new Kyrcznovian government officials wanted to offer their children—*their future*—a better education. That was something the 'mother country' could never afford to give them, so that was part of the new leaders' primary plans. And I was part of that plan. Me and about a dozen other English teachers." She raised her brows, lifted her palms. "But that all changed yesterday when the funds for the program were suddenly cut off." Her tone dropped to a grumble as she added, "They probably needed money for the new army or something."

"Did you have a contract?" he asked.

"Of course. But it's only as good as the piece of paper it's written on."

"But surely something can be done."

The passion in his outrage for her plight made her insides grow all warm and fuzzy. Sean Hudson really was a nice man.

"Surely they can be made to hold up their end of the deal they made."

Nicki nodded. "I could fight it. But that takes money. Lots of money. And more time than I have. I've decided the best thing for me to do is cut my losses. Find another job. Earn enough money to cover the travel expenses to my next teaching assignment."

"Which is where?"

The grin she tossed him was a sheepish one. "I have to find it first, then I can tell you where."

He shook his head. "But—"

"Look, it's okay," she assured him. "I've been traveling Europe, teaching English for five years. Ever since I graduated from college. This kind of thing has happened before. Not so suddenly, maybe. But it's happened. I'll survive. Something will turn up."

Creases of skepticism marred his forehead, and she was sure he was going to argue with her, but the waiter interrupted them with plates of food.

Scooping up a forkful of *halusky*, she commented, "Well, you know my troubles. Now it's your turn." Before she even had time to chew the small potato dumplings, she was holding a picture of Sean's "little girl" as he called the child he'd traveled halfway across the globe to adopt. Nicki listened as he summed up his story as quickly as possible; how he'd been told back in the States that his bachelor status was no problem, how he'd discovered the rules had changed, how he'd been encouraged to remain in the country with the hope that the government's dictum would be reverted once again. Finally, Nicki had to place her fork on the table. The knot of emotion that had formed in her throat made it impossible for her to swallow.

"I don't know, Nicki." His voice was a mere whisper. "I own my own business and that's why I've been able to stay these extra days. But I can't let my company go to hell in a hand basket. I just don't know how much longer I can wait for Child Services and the government to get their acts together. I go to see them twice a day. I explain to everyone who will listen that it's in Sona's best interest to go home with me." He shook his head. "But, so far, I haven't convinced anyone."

The pain and worry in his dark eyes wrenched her heart.

"Have you seen her?" Nicki asked. "Have they let you spend time with Sona?"

Sean shook his head, and his anxiety seemed to grow. "They say the adoption is too much in question to allow us to meet. To bond. They say they are only trying to spare the both of us the pain of separation. I understand. But, Nicki, I already have a bond. An emotional bond that started weeks ago. I'm already suffering the pain of separation."

His jaw clenched then, and just before his gaze slid away from her face, Nicki was sure she saw his eyes misting. This man was hurting. Badly. All for the sake of a little girl who probably didn't even know of his existence.

Yet.

His story, his *suffering*, roused something inside Nicki. Something she couldn't quite figure out. Something that moved her to act—swiftly, mindlessly—before she even had time to contemplate the consequences of her behavior.

"Well, Sean." The nerves jittering in her belly made her voice come out sounding weak and shaky. "If all you need is a wife, then I'd be happy to marry you."

Chapter Two

Nicki could not believe the words that had just somersaulted right out of her mouth. She'd parted her lips and the offer had twirled and flipped, making a perfect execution like an outstanding Olympic gymnast.

Oh, she knew why she made the suggestion of marriage. Her motivation couldn't have been more clear to her had it been the bright and blazing summer sun rising over the wild Kyrcznovian landscape. Nicki took a quick peek at the little girl's photo. Sona. The dark-eyed toddler was all alone in the world. The mere idea stirred highly emotional memories in Nicki. Memories that threatened to bring tears to her eyes, swallow her whole, if she were to tarry in them long enough.

Blinking, she shoved her way out of the dark thoughts.

Nicki didn't know Sona, had never met this tiny moppet, but Nicki felt an affinity for her nonetheless. If Nicki could help rescue one lonely soul…

This time her tone was stronger as she repeated, "I'll be happy to marry you, Sean."

He didn't speak, his wide brown eyes staring in disbelief. He was evidently as stunned by her offer as she. More so, even.

She suddenly felt buoyant, certain she was doing the right thing. "Gee," she said, trying to fill the awkward silence, "it's not like I'm offering to become your lifelong partner. You only need a wife for a while, right? Just long enough so that you can adopt Sona." She grinned. "Then we'll get one of those quickie divorces that some of those states in America are famous for." She lifted her hands, palms up. "Couldn't be more simple, don't you think?"

It took him several moments to respond. Finally, he said, "Why? Why would you offer to do this, Nicki? You don't even know me."

The intensity in his gaze made her

uncomfortable. "It's nothing," she told him, wanting to sidestep his profound query.

He reached across the table and took her hand in his, and the heat of his skin sent concentric shivers coursing across every inch of her flesh.

"It isn't nothing," he said quietly. "It's something. Something big. Bigger than you can ever imagine."

His fingers were strong as they clasped hers, and Nicki's heart began to race.

"So, tell me," he pressed. "Tell me why you would do something like this."

With her free hand, she swiped her fingers through her bangs and shifted her gaze to glance off across the dining room. These were nervous gestures, meant only to give her time to think before she spoke.

Sean wouldn't understand her motives. Then again, maybe he would. But did she really want to expose that much of herself to a total stranger? She didn't think so.

If he decided to take her up on her offer, then they would marry, she would go with him to pick up his new daughter, she might even go with them to the airport. However, soon, he and the little girl were going to fly off toward the West in a big plane... and Nicki would never see him again. So why should she bare the most painful part of her past to him?

She shouldn't, she decided, pressing her lips together in a thin line. Inhaling deeply, she leveled a cheerful gaze on him.

"Look, I can help you," she said simply. "So, let me."

Sean let out a small chuckle. "You know, the man from Child Services who rejected my adoption request offered to find me a 'sturdy wife'... for a fee, of course. A measly hundred bucks. Is that all a sturdy wife is worth these days?"

Nicki's mouth dropped open a fraction in horror and surprise.

"I turned him down," he continued, his voice flattening. "You see, years ago I decided I wasn't going to get married." His jaw tensed and his gaze clouded over as he added, "Ever."

Remaining utterly still, she silently wondered what could have happened to force him to come to such a conclusion. *Years ago*, he had said. Yet he seemed young. Older than she, of course, but still young. Early to mid-thirties, she guessed. Seemingly too young to be tainted against loving relationships and lifelong commitments. What had he been through to cause him to—

Sean chuckled again, evidently launching himself out of his fleeting-yet-all-absorbing moment of sadness. "However, marrying for the sole purpose of adopting Sona. Now, *that* I would do."

A few seconds of acute silence had them both feeling awkward.

"I think it's called a marriage of convenience," Nicki said, forcing her mouth to curl

into a smile.

"So, what's in this for you?"

His question took her off guard. She blinked. "For me?"

He nodded. "*If* I agree to this—and I'm not yet sure I do—how can you benefit? What can I do for you in return?"

Straightening her spine, Nicki pulled her hand from his. "I don't expect to benefit."

"But how fair is that?"

"Who said life is fair?" Her chuckle didn't hold much humor. "The predicament I'm in right now pretty much answers that question."

"Oh, yes," he murmured. "Your predicament. Hmmm... how about if I pay you for your trouble?"

Nicki's tiny jerk was totally involuntary, as if she'd taken a quick slap on the cheek. "I will not take money from you. That's not why I made the offer."

Lifting his hands, he rushed to assuage the insult he'd inflicted. "I wasn't suggesting you had." Sean reached up and toyed with his chin. "Okay... how about—" he spoke slowly and softly, as if he were voicing an idea as it formulated in his head "—if you let me foot the bill for all your travel expenses to your next teaching assignment? Plane fare, hotel, meals, the works."

"Oh, no." She leaned away from him, shaking her head. "I couldn't allow you to do that. It's too much."

"Nonsense. If it's going to be a true marriage of convenience, then it has to be convenient for us both, right?"

"B—but—"

She continued to protest, but he silenced her with a firm, upraised hand. "No buts," he said with a great deal of adamancy. He rested his elbows on the table. "Nicki, I've been sitting in this hotel for days. I had just about given up. You've given me hope. You've made an offer to make my dreams come true. If you do this, you'll make me a father. Sona's father. Don't you realize what that means?

To me and to that little girl. You've got to let me compensate you in some way. Travel expenses is the least I can do. The *least*."

He was persuasive, Nicki thought. With his talk of fulfilling dreams and becoming a father. Yes, he was very persuasive, indeed. Finally, the stiffness in her shoulders eased and she smiled.

"Well," she said softly, "I didn't really want to spend the next couple of months working as a waitress, anyway."

His eyes sparkled with excitement, and Nicki felt a thrill shoot through her at the thought that she was the one who had caused it.

"I can't believe it, Nicki," he said. "I'm really going to do it. I really am."

The delight she felt magnified a hundredfold. His sudden elation over tying the knot, after he'd so adamantly proclaimed his aversion to matrimony, made her feel all sunny inside.

"I really am going to be Sona's father."

Nicki's mouth went suddenly dry with disappointment. Of course, his excitement had been spurred by the anticipation of adopting his little girl. Nicki was silly to have thought anything else.

"Yes," she said, doing everything in her power

to stir up a little excitement of her own. "And I've found the means to get to my next teaching assignment. Wherever that will be."

His sexy mouth widened into a grin and he reached out his hand to her. "So, we have a deal? We're going to help one another?"

With only the merest hesitation, she took his hand and shook it. "Yes, we are," she agreed.

An odd and confusing cloud descended on her, and where it had come from she hadn't a clue. She had found a solution to her problem. The answer had come. Just as she had known it would. And as an added bonus, with that solution had come the opportunity to help someone. She should be feeling happy. Joyous. And she did. But she felt something else, too. A strange melancholy hovered at the edges of her excitement. Finally, she decided she was being ridiculous.

***

"Ah, love is so... how do I say it... *grand!*"

Nicki had only just met Viktor, the Kyrcznovian translator Sean had hired when he'd first arrived in the country. The young man had agreed to attend their wedding ceremony and act as the necessary witness. She found Viktor to be a tad too high-spirited. Of course, her opinion could have been colored by the doubt she was experiencing, along with the rethinking she was doing, regarding her participation in this scheme. Was she *really* doing the right thing in marrying a perfect stranger? Of course she was.

But then Viktor gleefully proclaimed to the world at large, "Love is wonderful."

The man's boisterousness—all his talk about love—grated on Nicki's already frayed nerves. And from what she could see, Sean was becoming just as agitated.

"I told you, Viktor," Sean said, his tone flat, abraded, "this has nothing to do with love."

Viktor's voice lowered as he said, "But, Mr. Hudson, it is to invite... how do I say it... ill omens to have a wedding day and not speak of the most powerful of emotions." After a momentary hesitation, he continued, "It does not have to be your love that I proclaim. It can belong to someone else. But it is only customary to exalt and glorify love and affection and devotion—" he lightly thumped himself on the chest "—all matters of the heart, on a day such as this."

The fog that had hovered over Nicki during each

and every one of the forty-eight hours that made up the official waiting period grew denser by the moment. Ill omens and a loveless marriage. Boy, that summed up this situation perfectly.

Why was she feeling so... doomed? she wondered.

It just didn't make sense. Glancing at Sean, she saw the apprehension that plagued him had him antsy, too.

Viktor plowed ahead, ever joyous. "Look there." He pointed at a man and woman sitting on a nearby bench. "There is love and commitment in the way they are holding hands. And there." He indicated another couple. "The kiss they are sharing is sweet and pure." Viktor threw back his head and inhaled heartily. "Ah, yes, love is very grand."

Sean only tossed him a frown.

"Ill omens," Viktor warned in a singsong voice. "And since you are not having the traditional celebration—"

"Those parties can go on for days," Nicki couldn't help but interject.

"—you must at least agree with me on this," Viktor insisted.

After an impatient sigh, Sean buckled. "Yes,

Viktor," he said, "love *is* grand. Does that fulfill custom?"

Viktor sighed. "It will have to do." Then he raised his brows at Nicki, waiting for a response from her.

"You're pressing your luck now," Sean grumbled at the young man.

All Nicki could muster was a tight-lipped smile. What did they expect from her? She was getting married... without fanfare, or flowers, without rings, or a frilly dress.

Even her plastic smile faded at *that* thought.

What was the matter with her? She and Sean had decided that keeping things simple would be the best way to go. Fanfare and flowers, rings and a frilly dress were for people who wanted to show their family and friends how they felt about each other. She didn't love Sean. He didn't love her. She knew that. So what was the problem?

But, a tiny voice complained, *didn't a woman have a right to expect a little hoopla on her wedding day?*

No, came a firm, silent answer, *she did not. Not under these circumstances, she didn't.*

As they went into the building that housed the Marriage Office, Nicki plastered the artificial smile back into place. The hallway was long and poorly lit, but she and Sean knew their way as they had come here to register the very same day she'd offered to marry him. The office had been busy then, just as it was busy now.

It seemed that the spirits of the citizens of Kyrcznovia were not in the least dampened by the civil unrest going on around them. On the contrary, the people of this country were very enthusiastic about the birth of their nation, and they were showing their ebullience and excitement in many different ways. Getting married seemed to be one of them.

Nicki, Sean, and Viktor were told to take a seat.

Sitting in the overcrowded waiting area among all the laughing, affectionate couples, Nicki could clearly see that love was the main reason these men and women had come here. Of course, there were at least a dozen other reasons why people got married. She'd lived in enough diverse cultures to know that. There were some countries where matches were still made by the parents of the young people who married. Those were more like lifelong business relationships, although many of the men and women eventually ended up developing a deep affection for the mate chosen for them. The women in those marriages might not have begun those unions feeling loved, but surely they felt needed... *wanted.*

That one little word was enough to turn Nicki cold. A shiver actually coursed through her, and panic set in. It was then that she felt Sean's intense brown eyes on her. She lifted her gaze to his.

Although there was no way he could know her thoughts, he evidently perceived something disturbed her. Maybe he would graciously decide to refuse her offer. Maybe it wasn't too late for her to get out of this... this foolish arrangement.

Sean's expression verged on distraught. He leaned close, whispering in her ear. "I know you're having second thoughts. I've sensed it all morning. And I feel just awful about it."

After momentarily averting his gaze, he sighed and looked her full in the face. "But if we don't do this... if we don't go through with this marriage, they're not going to let me have Sona."

The second the little girl's name passed his lips, Nicki reached out and touched his forearm. "It's okay," she assured him, not feeling at all confident herself. "I'm just a little nervous is all. I'll be fine." His smile was small, but his gratitude was as clear as the finest crystal.

It wasn't long after their brief conversation that

they were called before the man who would marry them—the Kyrcznovian equivalent of a U.S. Justice of the Peace. The nagging cloud of doubt and anxiety never left Nicki, although she was too busy explaining to Sean all that was being said to focus on her uncertainty. When the officiant asked them if they both were before him of their own free will, Nicki softly said, *"Ano,"* and then prompted Sean to answer yes also.

Even Viktor had questions to answer about the couple.

There was one lighthearted moment when Sean became a little tongue-tied with the Kyrcznovian words that had him "pledging his truth" to Nicki. Everyone chuckled, and after a second attempt, Sean got it right. Finally, they were pronounced man and wife.

"Well—" Viktor nudged Sean with his elbow "—kiss her, why don't you?"

The whole room grew utterly still. Her new husband turned to face her, then he looked from the *Sobash uradnik*—the man who had wed them—then to Viktor and then finally back to Nicki. For a moment, she thought he meant to forgo this particular wedding ritual. Her stomach churned, her gaze darting from his questioning eyes, to his lips and then back to his eyes.

She was desperately afraid he would kiss her. She was also desperately afraid he would not. And the opposing confusion and chaos of these thoughts had her mind whirling a mile a minute.

Sean leaned toward her, and suddenly his mouth was pressed to hers. His lips were firm, yet gentle, warm and—

The kiss was over almost before it began. She felt both relieved and utterly bereft. Lord, she'd never experienced such a jumble of emotions in her whole life.

"Let's go." His whisper was rough against her ear.

In a fog-filled tunnel, Nicki felt as if she were in the throes of an out-of-body experience as Sean shook the hand of the *Sobash uradnik*, smiling tightly at the man's proffered wishes for a lifetime of happiness in a language he didn't understand. After accepting some papers from the man, her husband took her elbow and steered her toward the door.

Her *husband...*

Nicki took a deep breath. She felt light-headed and shaky.

This was stupid! She shook the thoughts from her mind. She was making too much out of all these silly feelings swirling around in her brain, in her chest. But her emotions were so surprisingly strong. And thick. They seemed to congeal in her lungs, making it hard for her to breathe.

Nicki and Sean burst through the door, into the bright sunshine. She gulped in the afternoon air, trying hard to keep her composure.

"The people at Child Services are expecting us," Sean told Nicki. "You will come with me?"

"Of course," she said.

He turned to Viktor. "Well, my friend... I want to thank you for helping me."

"This sounds like... how do I say it... a goodbye."

Sean shrugged. "Well, Nicki can translate for me, so I thought—"

"Oh, no," Viktor protested. "I want to stick with you until the end. I want to meet that little girl."

The excited anticipation glittering in Sean's eyes tickled Nicki and dissolved all her dark, ominous feelings. This man's dream was about to come to fruition. She couldn't blame Viktor for wanting to be present when it happened. She was pleased to be a part of it, herself.

"Well, then," Sean told them both, "let's go get my daughter."

***

He paced the length of the room and back. "What's taking them so long?" Sean asked. "The paperwork for the adoption has been in order from the beginning. All they wanted was for me to have a wife. I have one. So what's the hold up?"

Concern and commiseration etched lines in Viktor's young face as he looked at the clock on the wall.

Nicki let her gaze follow her husband's every move. She feasted on the sight of him. After today, she would never see Sean again. She wanted some memories to take with her when they parted.

She wasn't stupid enough to believe that she'd fallen for Sean Hudson since meeting him in that restaurant a couple of days ago. Why, he was really still a stranger to her. All she knew was that he loved a little girl he had never even met. And that had been enough to convince Nicki that he was one extraordinary man. A man she wanted to help. And she had. She should feel good about that. So why then did she feel so conflicted?

"Do you think they're questioning the marriage?" he asked.

The fear tensing his body tore at her like sharp talons. "Why should they?" Lowering her voice, she remarked, "They have no idea that the two of us made a... a—" her tongue tripped over the word "—bargain." However, she had no clue what was actually happening behind the closed door of the office.

"They have sent someone to fetch your little girl," Viktor said, his tone more confident than his gaze reflected. "I am sure of it."

Sean continued his pacing; Nicki turned back to staring out the window.

The door of the waiting room opened, and the man from Child Services walked in with a dark-haired toddler in his arms. He crossed the room and wordlessly, without fanfare of any kind, handed the child over to Sean. The air was so still, so silent. Nicki could hear her own heart beating like a huge kettledrum.

"Sona."

The euphoria in Sean's whisper sent a chill racing up Nicki's spine. Joy and relief made his gorgeous eyes shine with welling moisture, and Nicki had to press her fingertips to her lips to keep from crying. Viktor, too, was highly emotional, his Adam's apple bobbing in his throat.

More paperwork was exchanged, and finally, the government employee bid Sean a curt congratulations and he left them.

Viktor came to Sean and Sona, smiled softly at the little girl, and touched her on the chin. "You're a lucky little girl," he said to her. "I wish you much happiness, Mr. Hudson."

"Thanks for everything, Viktor." The two men shook hands.

"If you are ever in my city again, you be sure to... how do I say it... look me up."

Sean nodded. "You can bet I will."

After tossing Nicki a wave of farewell, Viktor closed the door softly behind him.

A moment of awkward silence followed. Nicki saw that Sona looked uncertain, and she thought that was a very natural thing for the child to be feeling. This lovely dark-eyed little girl might feel lost right now, but Nicki knew it wouldn't be long at all before Sona's gaze would shine with adoration and love when she looked at Sean. The two of them would develop that strong father-daughter bond. Nicki was sure of it.

Approaching Sean, Nicki said, "You want me to walk you back to your hotel?"

He shook his head. "I'm going to wait here awhile. I want to give her time to get used to me." Nicki hid her disappointment behind a smile. "I understand." He wanted time alone with Sona. That was clear. "You're going to be a fabulous father, Sean Hudson."

Then he did something wholly unexpected. He reached up and gently caressed her cheek. The moment was poignant, special, and she savored every delicious second.

"This wouldn't have happened without you, Nicki."

Her smile broadened. "I was happy to help."

"You have my business card," he said. "You call me as soon as you find a teaching assignment. I'll see that you get there. First-class."

His unexpected generosity made her chuckle. "Aw, but I'm not a first-class kinda girl."

"Oh, yes you are, Nicki Willis."

Her smile waned when he used her last name. She felt a funny kind of sadness to realize he didn't think of her as his Mrs. But why should he?

"You're most definitely first-class."

She only stared at him for a moment,

languishing in the warmth of his touch. And for an instant, she felt needed. *Wanted.*

Emotion bombarded her, and fresh tears prickled her eyelids, splintering his image into a thousand shards of watery light.

Stepping away from him, she dashed the tears away before he could see her reaction. This wasn't about her. It was about Sean. It was about Sona.

After clearing her throat, she said, "I'm only glad I could help."

She looked from him to the little girl, and leveled her gaze on Sean's face once again. Then and there, she knew that she'd done the right thing in marrying this man, in helping him adopt this beautiful, parentless child. Nicki had never been more certain of anything.

Reaching out, she captured Sona's fingers in hers. "Your daddy's going to give you a good life." She then repeated the words in the child's native dialect.

A shadow of a smile tilted the child's lips for a fraction of a second before the cloud of confusion and fear returned to her expression with a vengeance. Sona would be okay. With a loving father like Sean, how could she be anything else?

Nicki's gaze was helplessly drawn to Sean. "You're her everything now."

His soft, quick inhalation was unmistakable.

"I've never been anyone's everything."

His adoring gaze was locked on Sona. For some strange reason, Dina didn't want to go. But it was time.

Unable to bring herself to say goodbye, she simply offered him a smile. And then she left him alone with his new daughter.

Chapter Three

There simply wasn't a more adorable, more precious child in all of the whole wide world. Sean might be exhausted from his day, but as he sat on the one chair in the cramped hotel room, his heart pounded furiously in his chest, emotion lodged firmly and thickly in his throat.

This was real. This was happening. He was a father. He was Sona's daddy.

His jaw clenched as he forced back the overwhelming disbelief threatening to engulf him. He needed to keep himself composed, relaxed. For Sona's sake. Several times since they had left the Child Services office earlier today, she had been on the verge of crying. Her tiny chin would quiver, her eyes had grown fearful and teary, yet in each instance he had been able to divert disaster by distracting her. Quickly. With whatever had been close at hand—a small chip of ice from his cup, a spoon from the dinner table, the new rattle he'd purchased for her. Boy, keeping Sona's mind occupied with new and interesting things was hard work.

But even with the difficulties, he was unable to get over how happy he felt at this moment, how completely joyous he'd been since the moment Sona had been placed in his arms. This adoption felt so right to him. So very right.

His daughter sat on the roll-away bed he'd had brought in by the hotel housekeeping. There hadn't been a crib available. Ah, well, he'd thought, they only had to make do for one night. They would be flying home to America—tomorrow.

Sona played with the new rattle, turning it this way and that, smiling tentatively whenever it made a noise. The inexpensive toy enthralled her, and Sean could easily see that she hadn't had access to many playthings in the orphanage.

He'd taken her shopping for a few things: two bottles, a new dress, a little nightgown and, of course, some diapers. He'd also bought her some toys. Just a few small, colorful items. He didn't want to have to carry a lot of stuff on the airplane. But his own favorite was the small, redheaded doll he'd bought... a doll that reminded him of Nicki.

Several times this afternoon the woman had breezed into Sean's thoughts. His gratitude for what she had done for him was so immense; he didn't think he'd ever be able to repay her. Well, he'd just have to see what he could do when she finally contacted him about her travel arrangements.

He gazed across the room, remembering how the morning sun had turned Nicki's hair to copper fire, wondering what would compel a woman to give so much of herself to him—a total stranger? She'd gone to great lengths to help him. She'd actually *married* him. He wondered if—

A bubble of baby laughter broke into his thoughts, and his attention returned to his daughter. He smiled, content to simply watch Sona play with her rattle.

Late that afternoon, Sean and Sona had stopped in the hotel restaurant for some dinner. The menu didn't cater to children at all, so he'd ended up special ordering several different kinds of soft-cooked vegetables and he'd mashed them with his fork. Sona had eaten like a voracious little horse.

He'd focused so much of his attention on feeding his little girl, the chicken Kiev and *kasha* he'd ordered for himself had grown stone-cold before he'd taken a single bite. But that really didn't matter, especially when he knew his new daughter's belly was full. However, being satiated, Sona had quickly lost interest in the food, the utensils, and the napkin, and she had begun to squirm. So Sean had had to gobble his dinner and quickly find something else to hold her interest. He just chalked it up as being one more thing a new parent must do: eat cold, hasty meals.

Bath time had been an experience. As he had washed from Sona the sticky remains of dinner, she had splashed and squealed with glee. Sean's shirt-front had ended up as wet as she by the time he'd gotten the soap rinsed off her.

All in all, it had been a long and hectic day. And although he was still experiencing the effects of the adrenaline high caused by his successful adoption, he had to admit he was glad it was time for bed. Because he was dog-tired.

The cot Sona sat on had seemed soft enough, but as soon as it had arrived Sean had realized that it was much too narrow for Sona to sleep on without the fear of her falling onto the floor in the night. So he'd done his best to barricade all three exposed edges of the mattress. He'd used the pillows off his bed, rolled up his blankets, too. And he'd found an extra pillow in the closet. He studied the soft enclosure he'd created for Sona and sighed. That should keep her safe.

The bare mattress he'd left for himself caught his attention and he couldn't help but grin. Heck, he didn't need a pillow. He could cradle his head on his arm. And he didn't need blankets. The summer night was warm. He doubted that he'd sleep much tonight, anyway, he was so excited. A spontaneous and utterly delighted chuckle rumbled deep in his throat, and the sound had Sona gazing at him with her huge, dark eyes.

She didn't seem half as frightened as she had earlier this afternoon. She handled being with strangers well, and Sean guessed that had come with her experiences since her parents had died. She probably never knew from day to day who would be caring for her. But he wouldn't be a stranger for long. Each day would bring him and Sona closer. He could feel it in his heart.

Sona tossed the rattle aside and gazed up at him. Then she rubbed her eyes with her tiny fists. Lord, but she was just too cute. She was tired. Any fool could see that.

"It's time to lie down, sweetheart." Speaking softly and approaching her slowly, he picked up the rattle and set it out of reach. Then he eased Sona back until she was lying down in the safe little nest he'd created. Her bottom lip quivered. Her huge, brown eyes welled with the biggest, wettest crocodile tears he'd ever seen in his life.

"It's okay, sweetie," he crooned. "It's time to go to sleep. You're tired. We've had a long day. Daddy's tired, too."

As soon as he'd uttered his new title, a joyous chill coursed across his skin. He was this child's daddy. He picked her up, cradled her head against his shoulder, but her tears continued. Sean slowly filled his lungs with the soft, baby scent of her.

"Shhh," he said. "Hush, now. It's okay."

"*Pisne*," she said, her crying making her hard to understand.

"What? You want your rattle?" He picked up the toy and gave it a little shake, but Sona only became more agitated.

She pushed away from him, her weeping developing into hiccupping sobs. Taken off guard by her struggles, Sean's eyes widened and he dropped the rattle, pressing his hand against her back so she wouldn't slip from his grasp.

"Whoa there," he said. Due to his surprise, his tone was louder than he'd intended.

Sona howled. *"Pisne,"* she repeated over and over between her sobs.

He placed her on the cot, and that calmed her. But only a little. She seemed to be expectant, waiting.

Soon, her tears continued to flow. And Sean felt suddenly inept.

Her distress magnified. She obviously wanted *something.*

"You're thirsty?" He ran to the bathroom where he'd placed a bottle filled with juice in the ice-packed bucket to keep it cold.

"Here, sweetie." He offered her the bottle, only to have her slap it away.

Again, she repeated the word he didn't understand.

Okay, she didn't want her toys. She didn't want a drink.

An idea came to him...maybe she was too warm. Immediately, he reached down and removed the fluffy pink knitted booties he'd bought her this afternoon.

Still, she cried.

He checked her diaper and found it dry.

Her sobs rang like loud, grating bells in his ears. Sean paused, rubbed the back of his neck, raked his fingers though his hair, his feeling of incompetence swelling with each passing moment.

It wasn't as if he'd thought becoming a parent was going to be easy. He'd known the responsibilities of raising a child would be immense. Even before he'd left America, he'd spent hour upon hour planning what he could do for this little girl when they finally became a family.

He'd clothe her, see that she ate a well-balanced diet. He'd care for her when she was sick. He'd laugh with her when she was happy. He'd teach her games. Catch lightning bugs on hot summer nights. He'd bake peanut butter cookies with her on cool autumn afternoons. They would stream Sesame Street and Blue's Clues and Wonder Pets. Learn the names of colors, and to count, and recite the alphabet. He'd hold the seat of her bicycle, run alongside her, as she learned to ride. And when she got old enough, he'd send her to the best private schools. He'd see that she got piano lessons and dance lessons. And if she didn't like playing or dancing, he'd sign her up for t-ball. He'd make certain she participated in any activity that interested her. He'd save money for her college fund.

These were only some of the plans he had made during the weeks preceding the adoption. But standing here, seeing his little girl sobbing with the want of... *something*. And him not knowing what it was she was asking for.

Sean thought his heart would rip clean in two. And then panic set in.

He closed his eyes and inhaled deeply, a dense shadow rolling over him, smothering him like a wet wool blanket. How could he have ever believed he could do this? How could he have thought he could even begin to tackle the enormous responsibility of this small child's life? His heart raced, but this time it wasn't caused by euphoria or joy or happiness—it was due to an overwhelming doubt in his ability to do right by this utterly vulnerable child.

When he raised his eyelids, his gaze fell on the redheaded doll he'd bought for Sona, the doll that had reminded him so much of...

Nicki. Her name whispered through his mind like a fresh, spring breeze.

Surely, she would be able to help him. She

would know what it was Sona was asking for. She would be able to stop his little girl's tears.

He snatched up his cell phone and made the call, but after three short beeps, the phone went silent. He tried twice more. Connectivity had been a problem every day that he'd been in this damned country.

Sona's cries wrenched his gut and ratcheted up his frustration. He needed help.

He swallowed, remembering that he knew Nicki's address. He'd picked her up earlier today in a taxi so they could be married.

Checking his watch, he decided it wasn't too awfully late. She would probably be up. *If* she was at home.

Refusing to think anything else but that she'd be there for him, that she'd be willing to help him, he picked up Sona.

"Let's go, honey," he told her softly, knowing full well she couldn't hear him over her crying. "Let's go for a ride."

Nicki sat at the table in the small kitchen of her tiny basement apartment. The cheese she nibbled on, along with the delicious and hearty seven-grain bread, was her dinner. She studied yet another online employment site, and every so often she'd absently reach up and fluff her damp hair.

Sharing a bathroom with the two other basement apartments wasn't all that bad. But Nicki didn't like to take too much time in the shower, so she only washed her hair every other day. Tonight was one of those evenings.

After swallowing the last bite of cheese, she wiped her hands on a cotton towel and then slowly, meticulously combed her fingers though her long, wavy tresses. She always let her hair air dry. The heat from a blow dryer only made the natural waves kink into frizzy curls.

A long sigh issued from her throat. All evening she'd busied herself with the most mundane tasks: straightening her already-tidy apartment, hand washing a few underclothes, taking a quick shower, eating her dinner, reading and re-reading the same job descriptions she'd found on the web.

Focusing on the ordinary, the routine, was keeping her mind tightly reined. Preventing her thoughts from wandering. To the craziness of the past couple of days. To her marriage to a man who was a complete stranger. Shaking her head, she realized that wasn't the entire truth. It wasn't thoughts of the marriage she was avoiding, but the stranger himself. The devastatingly handsome man with whom she had exchanged wedding vows.

Sean. Just thinking his name conjured in her mind a clear and vivid image of his chiseled, swarthy features.

She had known that, in marrying her, Sean Hudson had been using her. But then, she had *offered* herself to be used. She'd wanted to help him. No, she realized, she had wanted to help that little girl. The child with whom she had more in common than she cared to admit.

However, in working together with Sean to secure the adoption, Nicki couldn't help but feel she'd formed a kind of bond with him. It wasn't an idea that was totally ludicrous, was it? There were many reasons that people were drawn together. And she and Sean had found one. Little Sona.

Closing her eyes, Nicki effortlessly remembered Sean's powerful, dark gaze when he had thanked her for her help. He'd reached out to her. Touched her cheek. And even now, she tilted her head in some vain effort to recapture the feel of his strong-yet-tender fingers on her jaw, sliding along her neck. But all she met was empty air.

Her eyelids flew open. A vague, almost shadowy

fear churned in her belly. The emotion confused her, had her looking around the room, her gaze wide as she searched for something with which to busy her mind, some mundane task to occupy her thoughts, divert her attention.

She got up, took her plate and glass to the sink, washed them, dried them, and put them away on the shelf. But the strange foreboding remained in her stomach, making her feel as if she'd eaten, not a delicious dinner of bread and cheese, but a bowl of dry and tasteless clay that had lodged in the pit of her stomach in a hard lump.

This was absurd. She'd helped an orphan find a home. She'd helped a man adopt a child. She should realize the goodness in what she'd done and leave it at that.

But Sean had stirred in her some profound emotions—feelings she didn't quite understand. The undercurrent of attraction was clear, she realized. But then any woman would have found the man appealing. However, it was the fearful feeling, the shadowy apprehension that she couldn't fathom. It wasn't like she was afraid of Sean. No. That wasn't it at all. The feeling came from somewhere inside herself. Somewhere deep inside...

Nicki shook the thoughts away, rushing into the modest sitting room and snapping on the television. It was high time she put all this out of her head.

Sean Hudson had already moved on. She had better stop dwelling on the incident—on *him*—and do the same.

A knock at her door had Nicki automatically perking up. Rarely did she have visitors. It was probably Antonetta. The tea bags in her neighbor's cupboard seldom lasted to the end of the month. But Nicki didn't mind offering her friend a cup of tea. Especially tonight. This evening she would welcome the diversion.

The toddler's wails could be heard even before Nicki opened the door. The sound made her frown in confusion, but the sight of Sean and Sona on her threshold made her lips part in utter surprise.

"What's wrong?" she asked, as she tugged on his sleeve to get him inside. "What happened? Is she hurt?"

Sean's eyes were wide with panic. He shook his head. "She's not hurt. But she's upset. She wants something. Kept saying it. Over and over. I couldn't understand. She's been crying. And asking. For something."

"What?" Nicki asked above Sona tearful sobs. "What was she saying?"

Again his dark head shook. "Dunno. Peez-something." His frustration mounted.

Nicki soothed her hand down the toddler's leg. "Okay, baby doll, tell Nicki what you want."

Sona screeched, hiding her face in Sean's neck. "Lord, help me." His whispered prayer was accompanied with a quick glance heavenward. "Honey," he crooned to Sona, "it's okay. Everything is okay."

But the tension in his voice, in every muscle of his body, conveyed a far different circumstance to Nicki.

Sean's gaze implored her. *Help me*, it silently asked.

Touching Sona, or trying to take the child from Sean would only make matters worse, Nicki feared. She decided that even addressing Sona when the child was so upset was the wrong course of action. So she decided to focus her attention on Sean. If she could get him to calm down, then maybe Sona would as well.

"Sit down," Nicki quietly told Sean, pointing to an old, worn easy chair.

"I can't," he said.

He jostled the toddler, evidently hoping to rock her into a calmer state. Nicki sensed that the anxiety he was feeling was keeping him from realizing just how vigorously he was jiggling Sona.

"You *can*—" she took him by the sleeve of his shirt and directed him closer to the chair "—and you *will*."

He sat and the jostling stopped. But Sona's tears did not.

"What do I do?" he asked. "Tell me how to calm her. She's been crying for nearly thirty minutes. She's going to make herself sick."

"She looks so tired," Nicki observed.

"We're both exhausted."

He had faint circles under his eyes and his jaw was shadowed with the day's growth of beard. Nicki couldn't help but remember how clean and smooth his face had been that morning when they had stood together and...

Stop, she silently chided.

"I'm afraid I might have made a mistake."

His voice held enough doubt and insecurity to melt Nicki's heart. Crouching by the chair, she reached out and stroked his arm lightly, taking care not to touch Sona.

"All I wanted was to give her a good life," he

continued, miserably. "To make her happy. But how can I do that when I can't even tell what it is she wants?"

"You're going to be just fine," she told him. "You can't have expected every minute to be sunshine and roses. Especially at first. She's got to get used to you."

"But we did just fine this afternoon."

The three of them sat for a moment, Sean seeking solace from Nicki, Nicki trying to silently comfort him and Sona, who was releasing distressful sobs.

Then the little girl did the most extraordinary thing. She pressed her tiny palm to Sean's face and looked him directly in the eye. For a split second the room was filled with an utter and profound silence.

"*Pisne.*" Sona's voice sounded thick from her tearful spell.

Sean's gaze flew to Nicki. "There," he said. "That's it. What does she want?"

Nicki smiled. "She's asking for songs. She wants you to sing to her. Whoever put her to bed at the orphanage must have sung the children to sleep."

"Sing?" A crease marred his forehead. "I can't sing."

"Sure you can," Nicki encouraged him. "You must remember some simple songs from your childhood."

Sean shook his head, his frown deepening.

"How about the alphabet song?" she suggested. "Everyone knows that. Surely that's how you learned your letters."

He looked skeptical, but he began to sing the alphabet, his voice tentative, low, but velvety rich. Sona quieted down, sniffed back a hiccup or two and then cuddled up against his chest, plunking her thumb into her mouth.

The sight of this tall, muscular man cradling his tiny little girl in his arms, singing to her softly, made a lump of emotion swell in Nicki's throat. It was beautiful. Loving. Serene.

She hadn't expected to see Sean ever again. What contact she'd anticipated would have been over the phone or through e-mail once he'd returned to America. But here he was. In all his broad-shouldered, gorgeous glory. It was enough to make Nicki's heart flutter hard in her chest.

Before he'd finished a second repeated verse of the song, his daughter had fallen into a deep sleep. Sean finished the words, obviously unable to tear his gaze from Sona's peaceful face. Finally, he sighed. The immense relief expelled in that huge exhalation was clearly evident to Nicki. They sat for several moments in silence, both of them listening to Sona's steady, even breathing.

His deep-brown eyes were as intent and fixed on Nicki as they had been earlier that afternoon just before she'd told him goodbye. Nicki suppressed the shudder that coursed involuntarily up her spine.

Finally, Sean whispered, "Thank you. *Again.*"

Gratitude clearly overwhelmed him. She was frantic to somehow lighten the mood.

With that idea at the forefront of her thoughts, she cocked up one corner of her mouth into a lopsided grin. "Anytime," she quipped.

The seriousness in his expression didn't soften one iota. "Don't make light of this. If you hadn't been here to help me, to tell me what it was she needed, to figure out she was used to being sung to sleep—" he shook his head "—I don't know what I'd have done."

Softly, she tapped her fingers against his forearm. "It was nothing—"

"*Don't.*"

Sona stirred, and both Sean and Nicki grew stone-still. His eyes never left Nicki's, and in the end she became discomfited enough that she was forced to break their visual contact by turning her head away.

Finally, she lifted her face to his, surrendering to his solemn mood. "Okay. You're very welcome."

He didn't respond, simply continued to study her.

She felt the urge to squirm, but she didn't. Instead, she said, "You would have been fine, you know. You'd have figured it out. In time."

His thoughts were churning; she could see it in his expression. Her words seemed to spark an idea in him.

"In time," he murmured. Then he fell silent.

He pondered something, and she couldn't help but wonder what was going on in his head.

"Yes," she said. "You'll—'"

"*I will*," he interrupted her. "I'm sure I'll get it right. In time."

She smiled. She liked his confidence. Found it... very enticing.

The observation stopped Nicki mid-thought. Her smile faded. She had to stop this. Granted, he was handsome, he was giving and kind, he was doing something exceptionally worthy; he was the closest thing she'd ever met to the proverbial knight in shining armor. But that didn't give her a license to go all doe-eyed every time he opened his mouth. The best thing to do, she swiftly decided, was to simply ignore the silly attraction she felt for this man.

"Good," she told him, hoping that her tone didn't reveal the allure she was determined to suppress. "I'm glad you're seeing things my way."

"But," he continued, "until that time comes, I'm going to need your help."

"Excuse me?"

"I want you to come to work for me. I want you to fly home with me and Sona tomorrow. I want you to be there to help me understand Sona. I want you to teach her to understand me. Teach her to understand English, I mean."

Nicki frowned. "Sean you don't need me for that. Sona is just a baby. Toddlers are like little sponges. She'll soak up English in no time." Her insides began to quake at his startling request. "No time at all."

"You don't have a job," he continued to argue his point. "Let me provide you with one. You can be Sona's nanny. Her governess. Her teacher. My teacher. Call yourself anything you want. But come to work for me. We need you."

Her heart lurched against her ribs and her mouth went dry.

No, Nicki, a tiny voice said. *Don't even consider this.*

There was nothing for her in the United States.

Nothing at all. That's why she'd spent all her time in Europe since graduating from college.

"You don't even know me," she pointed out.

"I know enough," he said. "I know you're the kind of woman who put her whole life aside for two days in order to make a total stranger's dreams come true. You're a good person. Honest. True to your word. That's enough for me at the moment."

"B-but—"

"Nicki..."

The quiet desperation in his voice as he spoke her name sliced through the very words she was about to utter.

"...I *need* you."

Chapter Four

His plea was like a physical caress, and Nicki went utterly still as she waited for his words to brush warmly against her cheek. She knew very well that it was a juvenile thought. But still she remained motionless, waiting. Just waiting.

And while she was in that expectant and placid place her thoughts turned to chaos.

There is nothing for you in America. Nothing. That's why—

But Sean will be there. And Sona. And they need you.

You cannot get involved in this. You can't afford to travel to the States. You can't afford it monetarily. Or emotionally.

Frowning, Nicki didn't fully understand the implications of the unexpected, dark and whispery notion, but before she could indulge in further examination, other ideas pushed the shadowy concept aside.

But look at him, her brain whirled on. *He loves this child. He wants this little girl to accept him. Wants the two of them to become a family. How can you not help him?*

Easily, another more cynical thought crowded in. *Just say no. Do not allow yourself to become embroiled—*

But they need you.

At that moment, Sona stirred. And Nicki watched with rapt attention as Sean automatically lifted his big, strong hand, smoothed his flattened palm ever so gently, ever so lovingly down his little girl's back, comforting her, lulling her into feeling safe and secure.

Never in Nicki's life had she met a man who showed more tenderness, more unconditional love. Never had there been a man more worthy of having his most desired wish come true... that of becoming a daddy.

Like the wings of a tiny hummingbird, Nicki's heart beat frantically. She was stunned to realize that the attraction she'd felt for Sean—the fascination she'd thought she'd successfully repressed—once again reared up out of hiding like a hungry cobra, threatening to swallow her whole. And on the heels of the mesmerizing magnetism came that same vague fear she'd experienced before, too. A sort of dread that was both obscure and confusing. She swallowed, shoving the puzzling emotions from her.

No. *No*, she determined with silent force. This wasn't attraction she was feeling. This weak-in-the-knees emotion had to do with the connection she felt to Sona. The common bond they shared.

It was a flimsy lie, at best. But Nicki was in the perfect mind-set to grasp a tight hold on the thin half truth.

Sona had the chance of a lifetime here, the silent voice in Nicki's head continued to argue stubbornly. This little girl could have a family. A father who wanted her. Who loved her. Cared for her.

And Nicki could, once again, have a hand in making that happen.

For Sona, the two small words echoed across her mind. Then, nodding, Nicki looked Sean in the eye and said, "Okay. I'll do it. I'll go back to America with you."

***

The Philadelphia airport was crowded as Sean, Sona and Nicki made their way to luggage pickup. The three of them had ended up staying in Kyrcznovia for another day because there hadn't been a seat available for Nicki on the plane. She had suggested that Sean and Sona fly out as scheduled and she would meet them as soon as she could book a flight. But Sean had refused to leave without her. He'd given up his seats to an elderly couple who were on stand-by, and he'd somehow found a flight for all three of them today. Nicki couldn't begin to guess what the last-minute tickets had cost him.

"I'm a born traveler," she'd told Sean. "As a kid, I never stayed in one place for very long. And my teaching has taken me all over Europe."

Bogging herself down with lots of possessions just wasn't practical with her constantly-on-the-move lifestyle. The few bulky items she couldn't pack, she gave to her neighbor, Antonetta, who'd been happy to have them.

"I'm amazed that you've stowed your whole life into two canvas duffel bags," he'd observed.

She'd pointed out, "And a backpack."

He had chuckled, shaken his head and murmured something about never having met anyone quite like her. Well, that was okay, Nicki remembered thinking at the time, because she had never met anyone quite like Sean, either.

He'd entertained Sona through their long flight. He'd played patty-cake, peek-a-boo, and about a dozen other games he'd made up on the spur of the moment. When Sona had finally grown tired, Sean had sung to her softly, mostly nonsensical tunes that had neighboring passengers casting him odd glances, but the songs had only made Nicki smile endearingly.

There seemed to be a new boldness in Sean since Nicki had agreed to return to the States with him. Almost as if he'd had the intent and determination to be a good father to Sona, but with Nicki by his side to help him smooth over the rough patches of his initial journey into parenthood, he now had the confidence he needed to really and truly reach his desired destination.

The realization that she had helped to instill some faith in him made her feel really good. Kind of warm inside. Encouraging people, making them feel capable was part of her job as a teacher. She'd found that motivating her students with positive feedback and doing what she could to bolster their self-confidence only made them more excited about learning. Encouraging Sean had been easy. It was so obvious that he loved Sona and wanted to be the best daddy he could be.

However, Nicki didn't want Sean to become too dependent on her. So she had been very clear that she couldn't remain in America for very long. A month or so, two at the very most.

"Four to eight weeks," Sean had mused. "I think Miss Sona and I can get comfortable with one another between now and then."

At luggage pickup, Sean handed Nicki his sleeping daughter so he could gather together their bags. And soon they were in a hired limo, headed for his home in the suburbs.

"You work in Philadelphia?" she asked him, realizing that she knew very little about the man she'd married.

"Actually, I work from home, not too far outside the city."

The westernmost portion of the sky had turned a dozen different shades of vermilion as the hazy sun set low on the horizon.

"I design custom computer systems for small businesses," he added. "Technology is changing every day. Keeping up with those changes keeps me in high demand. I've created and updated systems for companies all over the United States. I hope to break into the foreign market soon."

"Sounds like you're off traveling a lot," she commented.

"Nah," he said, shaking his head. "With the internet, email, and my cell phone, I don't usually have to leave my office. I have an app that let's me attend meetings virtually. Of course, once in a while emergencies pop up and I'm forced to travel. But those are rare occasions."

"I see."

"Working from home isn't a big deal these days," he said, "I have the perfect setup to be a work-from-home dad."

He smiled, his white teeth glinting in the fading twilight, and his handsome face made Nicki's breath catch. A funny sort of heat began to curl inside her, low down, deep at her very core.

She glanced out the window at the passing scenery, taking a moment to quell the tendrils of awareness that had sprouted to life.

Tossing him a grin, she quipped, "Stay-at-home dad. Sounds like the perfect arrangement for you and Sona."

Sean chuckled, and the rich, happy sound vibrated in the quiet confines of the luxurious limousine. Nicki loved that sound, she decided, and an immediate sense of self-consciousness pervaded her. Thankfully, Sona chose that moment to awaken.

The toddler opened her big, beautiful eyes, blinked awake, and sighed. She pushed and shifted, struggling to a sitting position on Sean's lap.

"Well, look who's up." Sean gently moved aside Sona's bangs from her face. "Your nap was so long, sweetie, I'm afraid you won't sleep a wink tonight."

Nicki was grateful that his attention was focused on Sona. She desperately needed a moment or two to toss some cold water on the chaos plaguing her.

"That's okay, though," he continued, talking to his daughter. "We'll get into a routine soon enough."

The tenderness that tinged his voice as he spoke to Sona caused sudden tears to prickle Nicki's eyelids. She quickly turned her head and stared out the window. What on earth was wrong with her? First, she was forced to tamp down her growing attraction, and now the mere sound of his voice was causing her to well up with emotion.

She was exhausted from the long day of traveling. That's all it was.

The driver turned down a narrow, winding asphalt lane.

"We're here," Sean said. "Look, Sona. We're home."

Covertly dashing the heel of her hand against her moist eyes, Nicki etched a smile onto her mouth and took a slow, deep, steeling sigh. She was merely tired, she silently repeated the excuse, and the fatigue was getting the best of her.

His home was a beautiful brick colonial set so far back from the road that she couldn't see or hear the sparse traffic going by. In the ever-dimming twilight, she spied the outline of a building not too far away.

"Neighbors?" she asked.

He shifted Sona on his hip, directing the driver to leave the luggage on the porch by the door and then he gazed out to where she'd been looking. "No," he told her. "That's my barn. I keep two horses. My property butts up against a state park, so I can ride... if I get up early enough. I don't like to bother the hikers." With his eyes still trained on the barn, he said, "I have a cat around here someplace, too. Chunky doesn't come around unless she's hungry. I hire a man to take care of the animals, and the grounds. That way I'm free to work. Bob comes every day. If it hadn't been for him, I wouldn't have been able to stay in Kyrcznovia all that time. I'm sure he took good care of things while I was gone."

Two horses, Nicki mused, silently realizing that the property must be substantial. And being adjoined to a park would only increase the value of Sean's land. The limo he'd hired, with its soft leather seats and silent driver, had been the most opulent vehicle she'd ever ridden in. His business must be very successful in order for him to afford all this just thirty minutes outside a sizeable city, she thought, looking around her.

Sean glanced over the front lawn as the car pulled away down the lane. "The grass looks good. I knew I could count on Bob to take care of the place. I need to remember to thank him." He reached for one of her duffel bags. "You want to carry Sona? Or some of the bags?" She smiled, even though she doubted he could see her in the dusky night. "I'll take Sona and one bag. And please don't make it the one I over packed."

He let them into the house and headed right up the stairs toward the bedrooms.

"You'll stay in the room at the end of the hallway," he told her.

"The important thing is," she said, "which room is Sona's?"

"Ah..." Sean set down the bags he was lugging. "Right in here." He pointed. "The room has been ready and waiting for weeks."

The bedroom was just as cute as it could be, decorated in Mother Goose characters. Humpty Dumpty sat on a wall and Little Miss Muffet was there along with the happy-faced spider who hoped to share her curds and whey. Little Boy Blue was blowing his horn. And the Little Old Lady who lived in a shoe was tending her multitude of children.

Plush blue carpeting covered the floor and the furniture was white. The window coverings were pink. A small toy chest sat in one corner. Sean had designed the perfect child's room for his little girl, and Nicki was quick to tell him so.

"I can't take the credit," he admitted, taking Sona from Nicki and setting her down. "I had a decorator come in and do most of the work. But I did pick out the toys. I had a blast in the toy department."

Sona made a beeline for the rocking chair, and

with one touch she set it into gentle motion. She looked startled by the movement and turned her lovely doe-eyed expression first to Sean, then Nicki.

Both of them smiled at her surprised expression, then they broke out with soft laughter when Sona tried to climb onto the seat of the chair, but the rockers and the simple laws of gravity had her plunking down onto her bottom on the soft carpet. An instant of fear clouded Sona's eyes as she gazed at Sean.

"You're okay," he told her. "Don't you worry. You'll learn soon enough how to climb up there." Then he went and took her hand. "Let's go show Nicki to her room."

Even though the child didn't understand him, she curled her fingers around his. On his way out the door, Sean picked up the heaviest canvas bag with his free hand, then he led Sona to the end of the hallway.

"You and Sona will be sharing a bathroom," he told her, indicating one of the doors they passed with a nod of his head.

She grinned. "That won't be a problem. I've shared a bathroom with an entire floor of families."

She chuckled. "I've perfected the five-minute shower."

"Well, there'll be no need of that here." He went through the door of her room, set down her bag and flipped on the light. "There's plenty of hot water. Enough even for a long soak in the tub. Every single day, if you like."

The mere thought of a hot bath was so sinfully sensuous that Nicki actually groaned. "You have no idea how wonderful that sounds." When she opened her eyes, she thought she saw a fleeting sense of tension in Sean's jaw. However, on second glance, she didn't see a trace of strain.

She looked around at the pale-green and rich cream decor. "Nice," she told him. "Very nice."

"I hope you'll be comfortable."

The odd tautness in his voice made Nicki frown. Her gaze flew to his face, but he'd dipped his head, busying himself by picking up Sona and smoothing her little dress.

What had she done, what had she said, to cause the change in him? To induce the sudden tension she felt in the air?

"I'm sure I'll be fine." Her assurance sounded vague and far-off.

Sean walked to the door. "You get yourself

settled. I'll take Sona down to the kitchen and see if I can rustle up something for us to eat. There won't be much in the fridge. I've been gone quite a while. It'll probably be soup and crackers."

"I don't mind cooking—"

"No," he cut her off firmly, not bothering to turn back.

The sharpness in his tone made her spine straighten. He had never been short with her. A frown drew her brows together, her gaze on his back.

"Come on down after you've unpacked some of your things."

And then he was gone.

Confusion swirled around her along with the cool draft that poured into the room from the air-conditioning vent. What had happened? Why had things turned so tense?

Finally, she sighed. Maybe she was imagining it. Sean was surely just as tired as she. Maybe the long hours of travel were catching up to him, too.

She set her backpack on the soft cream-colored bedspread. The carpet and walls of the room were the exact same shade of soft green. The curtains matched the bed coverlet.

Calmness. Serenity. That's what she felt just standing in the middle of the room.

Nicki guessed that Sean had had the room professionally decorated, just as he'd had Sona's. The understated elegance was very nice, indeed. Nicer than any place she'd stayed in recently, that's for sure.

From the backpack she pulled out her hairbrush and comb and placed them on the dresser. She glanced up into the mirror. The hours of getting from Kyrcznovia to America had taken their toll on her. Mascara was smudged beneath her eyes, her hair a mess. Rather than unpack her clothes, she opted to go into the bathroom and freshen up a bit. She'd never been a vain person so she didn't fully understand this sudden urge to look nice. However, she couldn't help but suspect it had something to do with the man waiting for her downstairs.

Nicki went down the steps, following her nose toward the kitchen. She'd washed her face, brushed her teeth and run a comb through her hair. She'd applied a touch of fresh mascara. The short time she'd spent in the bathroom almost made her feel like a new woman.

When she entered the kitchen her attention was

immediately captured by the broad expanse of Sean's back. His shoulder muscles flexed and relaxed as he worked over a skillet at the stove. The small movement was mesmerizing. Nicki's pulse quickened. She forced herself to breathe slowly, evenly. Then she closed her eyelids, silently counting to five.

When she opened her eyes, she looked around her rather than at Sean. The kitchen gleamed with white cabinets and chrome appliances. It was a large, farmhouse-style room, wide-open and spacious. Finally, when her heartbeat had slowed to a more normal rate, she proceeded further into the room.

"Omelettes." She smiled as she watched Sean scooping the fluffy eggs from the pan.

"Yes," he told her. "There was no soup on the shelves. I hope you like eggs. It's about all we have. I'll have to go to the store tomorrow."

"I'm so hungry, I'd eat practically anything." Nicki was pleased that he seemed more relaxed than he had upstairs. His sudden snappish mood seemed to have passed. She was also glad she'd overcome her own bout with... well, whatever it was that had plagued her just a moment before.

The toaster popped, and she automatically went to pull out the bread slices.

"I found a loaf of bread in the freezer," he told her. "I hope there's butter in the fridge. Would you take a look?"

While they spent a few more moments preparing the simple meal, Sona concentrated on eating the raisins that Sean had placed on the tray of her high- chair.

"Mmm," Nicki commented when they sat at the table together. "This is delicious. Light and fluffy."

"I whip a teaspoon or so of water into the eggs to keep them moist while they're cooking."

"And the cheese." She was silent a moment as she marveled at the taste.

"Swiss." He grinned. "Although I had to cut the hard bits off." Then he cocked his head. "You look like you haven't tasted—"

"I haven't," she admitted, only just able to quash the nearly delirious groan hovering on her lips. "For *years*. The cheese that's most readily available in the backwoods of Europe is made from the milk of sheep. There's some goat's milk cheese. But no Swiss to be had." She took another moment to chew. "This is *so* good."

Sean laughed. "Gee," he said, "you're pretty easy to please."

Realizing how silly she must look to him, her face flamed. Then she broke out laughing herself. She shrugged and admitted honestly, "I forgot what I'd been missing." She scooped up another bite of omelette. "This really is good." Her mouth closed over the fork.

After the last bite of egg had been consumed, along with the last crumb of buttered toast, Nicki said, "Why don't you let me clean up? I'll watch Sona and you can go have a shower."

He looked at her a moment. "You know, I think I'll take you up on that offer. Just put the dishes in the dishwasher. I'm going to go look in on the horses, see if I can find that cat of mine, and then I'll take a shower."

Later, after Sona had been bathed and dressed in her pajamas, the three of them sat on the floor of the toddler's bedroom. They had pulled out the wooden blocks Sean had bought weeks earlier, and he and Nicki stacked towers that Sona delighted in knocking down. Soon, though, Sona sat down and concentrated on making towers of her own, stacking one block atop the other.

"So," Nicki said, "now that you have Sona home,

do you want to have a party? To introduce her to your family and friends. I'd be happy to help."

"There's no need for a party." He let a block roll off his palm onto the pretty blue carpet. "I have no family. Well, no close family. I was an only child and my parents died in a boating accident eight years ago."

"Oh, Sean," she breathed. "I'm sorry."

He accepted her condolences with a small nod. "And the friends I have I made through my business. They're scattered all over the country. And we're not close enough to celebrate something as personal as this."

How lonely he must be, Nicki thought. No family. No close personal friends. She wondered if he had a girlfriend, someone on whom he could depend during this new phase in his life, but she didn't have the courage to ask. From what he'd said, though, he didn't have anyone in whom he could lean on... confide his doubts, his fears, or share his triumphs and joys.

With her mind still churning over his circumstance, she asked, "So there's no one you need to notify about Sona's arrival into your life? Nobody you want to celebrate with?"

Something in her tone had him looking at her,

his brow slightly furrowed. "Don't be feeling sorry for me. My life is just as full as I want it to be. I have my work. I have my horses. My cat." He grinned. "And now I have a daughter. My world has expanded quite nicely, if you ask me."

But you need someone, she wanted to say. You need a friend. A companion. A mate. A *wife*.

Remembering how she came to be here, the thought immediately narrowed, focused like a sharp ray of light. A *real* wife. Someone who would be around to help you raise Sona.

Placing herself in the role she was conjuring never entered her head. She was Sean's wife, yes. But only for the moment. She was a temporary spouse. *Very* temporary. Her footloose life-style wouldn't permit anything else.

However, once their marriage was annulled, he should really try to find a woman who could and would spend her life helping him make a happy home for Sona. That's what would be best. For Sona. And for him.

Nicki wanted to tell him all these things. She wanted to discuss the cons of what she saw as the isolation he'd set up for himself. He might think his world was open enough, full enough, but she couldn't fathom how that could be true. However, she couldn't bring herself to tell him her thoughts. She just didn't know him well enough. Didn't know how he'd react to unsolicited advice. So she'd have to wait awhile. Until she got to know him just a little better.

Hours later, Nicki lay awake in her bed, staring up at the ceiling in the dark. Her exhaustion had had her yawning in Sona's room, and Sean had urged her to go to bed.

He expected Sona to be up late, seeing as how she'd taken such a long nap during the trip home.

When Nicki pointed out that Sean must be just as tired as she, and then offered to stay up with Sona, he'd gently rejected the idea. He was Sona's dad now, he'd proudly reminded her. He was the one who had to get used to the long, sleepless nights that other single fathers must surely be forced to endure.

He actually seemed eager for the experience, Nicki realized. So she had gone off to bed. However, once there, she couldn't sleep even though she was bone weary. She tried reading. Tried listening to slow, soft tunes on her iPhone's Pandora app. But nothing seemed to help. After what felt like at least a couple of hours of tossing and turning, she finally got up, grabbed her robe, and headed toward the door. What she needed, she decided, turning the knob, was a cool drink of water from the kitchen.

Moonlight streamed in through the bathroom window, casting long shadows in the hallway. She saw Sean at Sona's door.

"Did she finally fall off to sleep?" Nicki whispered, the darkness causing her to move closer than usual just so she could make out his face.

He smiled and nodded. "She looks like a little angel in that crib."

Nicki remarked, "She *is* a little angel."

"My little angel." He said the words almost to himself, then he focused his intent gaze on Nicki. He was quiet, reflective, as he looked at her in the dark stillness for several seconds. Reaching up, he captured her chin in his fingers. "And she's with me all because of you."

His fingers were warm against her skin. His touch sent adrenalin shooting through her, and her heart pounded. She studied his eyes. Those profound, sable eyes.

She wanted to blink. To look away. But she simply couldn't. She was lost.

"I was in there rocking her," Sean said softly, his fingertips sliding, like heated velvet against her flesh, "and it all just came flooding back to me again. I owe you so much. So much, I'll never be able to repay you."

Her gaze left his only long enough to watch the tip of his tongue sneak out to moisten his sexy lips.

"I only wish there was something I could do to let you know how grateful I am."

The silence that followed was so extreme, so penetrating, that Nicki was certain she'd never experienced anything like it in her entire life. Something was about to happen. Something wonderful. Or something terrible. She didn't know which.

The moment hovered on the very edge of time, and she couldn't decide if the cadence was quickening... or slowing. All she knew for certain was that she was trapped, hypnotized, unable to speak, unable to move, as she waited for the something that was most surely coming.

Then he moved. Not away from her, but toward her. And all Nicki could do was close her eyes and hold her breath.

Chapter Five

Searing heat. That was the one and only sensation of which Nicki was aware when his mouth closed over hers so possessively. Surely her lips would be blistered by his. White-hot, like the burning sands of some distant, sun-baked desert.

Then, slowly, other perceptions seeped into her hazy thoughts. The soft moisture of his kiss tempering the blazing fire. The silken feel of his tongue toying languidly across her lips. When she didn't immediately bid him entry, he lightly, erotically nipped at her bottom lip with his teeth, and it was this nibbling that had her emitting a soft but audible groan.

Almost of their own volition, her arms reached

up and slid around his neck. Her fingers entwined themselves in the short, downy hair at the back of his head, pulling him closer. His kiss became more ardent, more demanding, and she opened herself to him, parted her lips so he could venture inside the tender recesses of her mouth.

The desire that shot through her was so pure, so stunningly unadulterated, she was certain she would be scorched to the very soul. She clung to him for dear life, her knees having grown weak and wobbly, and the scant distance she traveled in leaning closer to him changed everything. Heightened the sensations she was experiencing. Snuffing out all her thought processes. Until all she could do was *feel*.

His rock-hard thighs against hers. The solid mass of his chest pressed tight against her breasts. His hands on her face and the small of her back. The heat of his body penetrating her clothing. She breathed in his sweet breath. And he breathed in hers. Again she moaned against his mouth.

Sean spoke. Some breathless, whispery proclamation that roused her, nudged her out of her passionate stupor, but not soon enough to have heard him clearly.

What had he said? she wondered. Had he murmured a curse? Whispered her name? What?

She blinked, and then realized that he'd pulled away from her several inches. He stared at her, shadows cast across his features obscuring his expression.

Giving a dry swallow, the hair on her arms rose as she was thunderstruck with a fear so sudden, so intense that she was barely able to suppress her startled cry. She shoved herself away from him, confused and filled to the brim with this vague and terrible dread.

"I'm sorry," he murmured.

She only looked at him with what she knew were huge, panicky eyes, feeling like a wild animal that had been cornered by a vicious hunter. She had to escape. She must flee.

"Nicki..." he began softly.

For some unknown reason, the regret she heard in his voice only seemed to magnify the panic whirling inside her. Before he could speak—she *must not* give him the opportunity to say another word—she turned on her heel, rushed blindly into her room and shut the door.

***

The horse's muzzle was like velvet. Nicki ran her fingers lightly down the coal-black nose, whispering a soft hello to the animal.

She'd been standing at the stall, intending only to take a quick peek at Sean's horses before going inside to make the morning coffee. However, while standing there, her thoughts had become sidetracked. She'd tarried so long the horse in the stall had approached her, rubbing the side of its face against the slatted gate, wanting—Nicki guessed—a little petting.

"What a pretty boy," she cooed.

The animal's coat was black and shiny as polished jet, glistening in the morning sunlight that streamed in through the large double doors of the barn. His shoulders were massive, his mane quite thick. And the horse's tail was so long it nearly brushed its back hooves. When the horse had first approached her, Nicki had felt hesitant. But it had nickered a greeting and was content when she began to cuddle him a little. Now feeling comfortable with her company, she let her mind continue to wander.

How on earth had she and Sean ended up kissing last night? That was the very last thing she'd expected... no, that wasn't true. At the very final moment, she'd known something had been about to occur. But a kiss? That hadn't been something she had *wanted* to happen.

But since it had, why had she panicked the way she had? Why had she felt so... filled with fear?

It wasn't as if she'd never been kissed. She was twenty-six, for goodness' sake. She'd had dates with men. Not a great deal of them, granted. But she'd had some. And she'd had her share of goodnight kisses, too.

So why the overwhelming anxiety?

Thinking about it only made her head begin to ache. The fear that had walloped her last night really didn't matter, she silently concluded, pushing the disturbing thoughts away. What mattered was that she *had* to keep her relationship with Sean on a friends-only basis, easy and casual. Europe was her future. She had classes to teach, children to instruct. She simply couldn't get involved....

She shook her head at the unfinished thought.

She'd have to tell him, she decided. She'd have to go over the ground rules they had laid out when she had agreed to travel home with him to become

Sona's nanny. She'd have to make her intentions crystal clear.

"Morning."

Nicki started, turning to see Sean standing in the doorway, the bright morning sun behind him. He came forward and the horse nodded its head in obvious excitement. Nicki backed a half step away from the stall.

"Hello," she said, the air in the high-ceilinged building feeling suddenly too close.

Sean handed her one of the mugs of steaming coffee he carried. Then he watched her inhale the rich aroma. She looked beautiful in the morning light with the sun turning her hair to flaming copper. Something deep in his gut stirred, but he clamped a tight, controlling lid on it.

He knew what was vexing him. Desire. He'd felt it early on last night when she'd groaned so deliciously in response to him telling her she could take a nice, long bath. The innocent sensuality in that sound had done something to him. Had provoked a hunger that had threatened to consume him. He'd fought the need, pushed it back. But in doing so, he'd ended up acting short-tempered toward Nicki. There was no doubt she'd noticed it.

And then there had been that kiss.

The kiss they had shared last night should never have happened, he reminded himself for what felt like the thousandth time. Nothing good could come out of it. For her. Or for him. He'd come out here to apologize. To promise that his behavior last night would not be repeated. And with the way she'd run from him last night, he was sure she'd be happy and relieved to hear all the things he intended to say to her.

"Thanks," she told him. And then she took a little sip, her milky-white throat convulsing delicately as she swallowed. The light, flowery fragrance of her skin rose up in his mind. Sean blinked, quickly focusing his gaze and attention elsewhere.

"I see you've met Pepper."

"So that's his name," she said.

Sean nodded. "Yeah, he came with the name when I bought him. He's a Morgan."

She frowned.

"Morgan is a breed," he told her, reaching out and running his palm down Pepper's powerful neck. "Originated in Massachusetts, actually. They're pretty easy to spot with their short, broad heads and thick necks. I felt that even though he's pretty independent, he's docile enough to make a good riding horse."

"So, he's mild-mannered?"

Sean smiled. "With a name like Pepper, you might not think so. But he's gentle."

"He's beautiful."

Not as beautiful as you. The thought whispered through his brain, stunning him, and he swore silently.

He'd told himself over and over last night as he'd tossed and turned that it was completely normal for him to feel physically attracted to her. She was a gorgeous redhead. A man would have to be stone-cold dead in his grave not to think her beautiful. However, he refused to ruin his arrangement with her. She'd made it clear she wouldn't be staying around. And that fit his purposes just fine.

But even if she hadn't stated clearly in no uncertain terms that she had every intention of returning overseas, he still wouldn't want to grow too close to her. He liked her too much. Thought she was too nice a person to have her life messed up with his emotional baggage.

"How about this big fellow?"

Nicki's question jerked Sean to attention. He saw that she'd crossed the barn to the opposite horse stall. She clicked her tongue, calling Blaze to her, but the horse remained standing at the far wall.

"Blaze can be a little shy," he said. "He'll do better once he gets to know you."

The silence that followed, along with his quick glance at her tight expression, made Sean aware that she was feeling just as awkward as he.

Evidently noticing the difference in the two horses' builds, she asked, "What breed is he?"

"Quarter horse. The name comes from a quality test established by the original Virginian breeders and had to do with the horses' ability to race a quarter of a mile."

For a few cumbersome seconds, she looked as though she was at a loss for something to say. Finally, she commented, "You know a great deal about your animals."

He shook his head. "Not all that much. I do know they're beautiful and graceful creatures." He offered her a stiff, lopsided smile. "That's enough for me." Another stilted silence followed. They sipped their coffee, but it was clearly evident that they were both feeling the strain of the drawn-out quiet.

"Sona's still sleeping?"

"Yes," he said, eagerly jumping at this change of subject. And then he placed his hand on the monitor attached to his belt. "I can be up in her room in a moment's notice. Lickety-split."

She smiled at the comment he had hoped would thaw the chilly atmosphere between them.

Softly, she said, "I haven't heard that phrase in years."

He knew what needed to be done. What needed to be said. And he had no idea what he was waiting for.

"Nicki, listen," he began, hesitancy making his voice catch. He gave a little cough and tried again. "About last night."

Her grip on the coffee mug tightened, her gaze automatically dipping to the hay-strewn floor.

"I don't know what got into me," he told her. "It was all my fault. And I apologize. I want you to know that... well, that kind of thing won't happen again. I need you. And Sona needs you. I was crazy to... do what I did. Wrecking our arrangement is the very last thing I want to do. So I hope you'll accept my apology. And my promise that it won't happen again."

When she didn't immediately respond, Sean felt

that maybe she was looking for explanations along with his regrets and promises.

"I, ah..." he stammered. "All I can say is that it was late. And we'd spent all that time traveling. And then I was up with Sona. I was tired."

Her gaze flew to his. "We were *both* tired. I'm really sorry, too."

The contrition in her tone took him aback.

"You have nothing to apologize for," he told her. "I was the one at fault. I take full responsibility. I feel just awful about it."

"B-but... like you said, it isn't going to happen again."

He nodded, relieved to see that she was as eager to put this behind them as he. "You have my word on that."

She smiled then, and it was as if the morning sun had just broken over the horizon.

Sounds of Sona stirring came from the monitor.

"Looks like my little girl is up," he said. "I'd better go get her."

"I guess I could fix us some toast—" after a moment's hesitation, she grinned broadly "—but I have to admit, I'd much rather come and help get Sona dressed for the day. I *am* supposed to be the nanny, you know. I should do something to earn my keep."

Relief flooded through him when he realized that his apology had so thoroughly cleared the awkwardness from the air. Thankfully, it seemed their relationship was back on the right track again.

"You'll be doing plenty," he assured her. "I've got a feeling Sona's going to be wanting to know a thousand different things about her new home. I'm just glad you'll be around to help me introduce her to everything."

They headed toward the house, side by side, an apparent, almost lighthearted spring in both their steps.

***

The days of that first week slipped into a laid-back routine. Sean worked odd hours in order to spend most of his time with his new daughter. He'd spend some time on his computer before the sun rose and work several hours before Sona even awoke. When the toddler went down for a nap, he'd head once again to his office to make calls. Or if he had work that needed his immediate attention, he'd place Sona on the floor of his office to play with a pile of colorful blocks or other toys.

During the times when his employees or clients needed immediate attention, Nicki offered, time and again, to take Sona outside so he wouldn't be disturbed. But Sean had declined. His reasoning had been that his daughter had to get used to the idea that her new dad worked from home. If he allowed Nicki to care for Sona now, what would he do once she had flown back overseas? No, he'd said, it was best for Sona to get into the pattern of playing in his office when he needed to be at his computer or on the phone. And Nicki had to agree. Of course, he'd told her, she was more than welcome to join in with Sona's fun on the office carpet, and Nicki always did.

She'd met Bob, the groundskeeper. He was a kind, elderly man who arrived every morning to feed and groom the horses, and then he'd cut the grass or spend a bit of time weeding the flower beds. He was always gone before noon.

Nicki found over the week that life took on a comfortable rhythm. She spent lots of time with Sona each morning, turning their play time into opportunities for the child to learn English. While Sona napped, Nicki searched the internet for available teaching jobs in Europe. Sean was always busy in his office and Nicki was often left to her own devices which was just fine with her. She'd do a little laundry or take a long walk, read a book or watch a little television. American TV, with all its choices, made channel surfing something that could easily become addictive.

The friendly atmosphere she and Sean had developed was great, right where it should be. They laughed together, ate together, and played with Sona together, neither of them having to worry about that bothersome complication called attraction.

Not that she found him any less attractive now than she had before he'd kissed her. To say that would be a bold-faced lie. He was handsome and intelligent... and he loved little Sona to distraction. *That*, Nicki guessed, was his most appealing trait.

When Sean chuckled at his little girl's antics, Nicki thought a more charming smile, a more delectable laugh, couldn't possibly be found.

Yes, she had to admit that he was the most handsome man she'd ever met. And she felt free to acknowledge that to herself now... because of his promise to keep things on a "friends only" basis.

When he'd explained that his kiss had been all

due to the fact that he'd been overtired, she remembered admitting they had *both* been exhausted, and she felt the need to explain her own eager participation in the passionate event. However, the important thing was that he'd assured her it wouldn't happen again.

He hadn't kissed her because he'd felt attracted to her. For some reason, knowing that allowed her to admire him from afar, without suffering that confusing and dark anxiety she'd felt before. She delighted in watching him with Sona. Or when he was deep in thought in front of his computer screen while she and Sona played quietly on the carpet. And he was a magnificent horseman, his powerful thighs flexing as he cantered Blaze in the enclosed paddock. She loved looking at him.

She did feel as if she was a help to him. At eighteen months of age, Sona didn't know all that many words. However, the child did know some. And she was bright and inquisitive and loved to communicate. So Nicki was happy that she was able to interpret the few phrases and words that Sona spoke. Soon, she hoped the toddler would begin to express her wants and needs using more English.

"Hey—"

Sean's voice had her looking up from the magazine she'd been paging through.

"Sona's up from her nap. How about a trip to the mall? We've been cooped up in this house long enough."

Nicki grinned, tossing the magazine aside. "I'd love it!" She stood up, instinctively smoothing out the wrinkles of her long skirt. "I haven't been to a big, glorious American mall in... *years*."

Sona enjoyed a bottle of chilled apple juice on the drive to the shopping center. When Sean pulled the car into a parking slot and cut the engine, Nicki looked at the huge building and felt a thrill shoot through her. Like many women, she loved to shop. But there was nothing like this in the small, Eastern European countries in which she'd worked for the past five years. Besides that, her meager paychecks allowed for no extravagance whatsoever. Her money was strictly spent on necessities alone: food, rent, clothing... and the only clothes she bought were sturdy items to replace those that had become worn.

Sean buckled Sona into a brand new stroller. The child looked about her, seeming to marvel at the contraption.

"Every experience seems so awe-inspiring to her," Sean noted.

Nicki nodded. "A lot of that has to do with her age. Toddlers are just normally curious. But some of it, I'm sure, comes from the fact that she was probably born into a poor family. Otherwise, she'd have found a home with relatives when her parents died. Sona's probably never ridden in a car. Or any kind of motor vehicle. She's probably never been strapped into a stroller and wheeled around. So all of this stuff is new."

Sean grinned. "It's almost like she's in one big amusement park."

"Something like that," Nicki agreed.

They went into the cool confines of the building, and Nicki couldn't suppress the smile that spread across her mouth.

"You can't imagine how wonderful this is," she breathed, gazing around at all the colorful window displays. There was a department store selling bold-colored women's clothing. Another store sold candles in every scent imaginable. Another, books of every description. There was a candy store wafting the delectable aroma of chocolate, and a jewelry store with diamonds and gold glittering under blazing lights. And that was only within eyesight of the one small wing where they had entered the building.

Tucking her bottom lip between her teeth, Nicki openly gaped at the colorful fashions displayed in the window of the apparel shop.

Sean's laugh drew her attention.

"You look like a kid with her nose pressed up against the glass of a toy store."

Nicki couldn't stop the chuckle that welled up from inside her. "I *am* like a kid in a toy store. You have no idea how different shopping is over there."

She knew he understood she was talking about the countries where she'd lived and worked for the past few years.

"You're right," he said. "I do have no idea. So tell me."

"Well," she began, "the economies of most of the Eastern Bloc countries where I've been teaching are poor. Goods are hard to come by. Up until just a few years ago, women sewed or knitted their own clothing. Some still do. And with the family income coming in at around two to three hundred dollars a month, there isn't much money for luxury items such as satin nighties or silk blouses. Those kinds of things can't even be found. Sturdy. Durable. That's what people are forced to focus on." She chuckled. "Kind of takes some of the fun out of shopping."

"I can imagine," he said.

"And some very necessary items can be extremely hard to find," she continued. "When I first moved to Kyrcznovia, it took me two full weeks to find a small refrigerator. And that one was secondhand."

"Wow. I had no idea. It makes me feel a little guilty for having so much... stuff."

"Don't," she told him. "You work hard for your money. Just be grateful for all that you have."

"I'll try to keep that in mind." He absently rocked the stroller back and forth to keep Sona happy.

A particularly gorgeous green silk blouse caught Nicki's attention and she sighed. "It's so pretty."

"Let's go in," he suggested. "You can try it on."

"Oh, no." She waved aside the idea. "I can't possibly afford it."

"So?" he said. "When has that ever stopped a woman from trying on pretty clothes?"

Nicki had to laugh. Finally, she shrugged, her blood pumping with the anticipation of feeling that silky fabric between her fingertips. "Okay. Let's go." Succumbing to his suggestion only had her feeling decadently evil... in the most fun sort of way.

The blouse was heavenly against her skin. She slid her arms into the fluttery, capped sleeves, and as she fastened the buttons, she glanced in the mirror at herself. The color was so rich. Striking, even. Clothing dye of this quality simply wasn't available in the back hills of Kyrcznovia. She pulled on the complementary taupe walking shorts, zipped them and fastened the leather belt. Then she stepped out of the fitting room.

"Wow!" Sean remarked. "You look great."

She flushed at his compliment. "Thanks."

The sales lady offered her another coordinated outfit to try.

"Oh, no," Nicki politely declined. "We're just having a little fun."

Sean's brows raised. "Is there any reason we shouldn't go on having a little fun?" he asked.

He was impossible, she thought. She cocked her head a fraction and tried to stare him down, but he refused to budge.

"Okay," she finally whispered, heaving a sigh of surrender as she took the proffered outfit from the woman.

Four times she went into the fitting room. She

tried on two shorts outfits, one paisley dress in turquoise, and a black skirt and royal-blue blouse combination. Sean raved about each one. And Nicki just beamed. She couldn't help it. His appreciation made her feel feminine. Pretty. This was something she hadn't experienced in quite some time.

Finally, she came out of the fitting room in her own clothing. "No more," she pronounced firmly.

Sean just chuckled at her. He turned to the sales lady. "Wrap them up."

"No, Sean!" Nicki was horrified. She hadn't tried the clothes on with any intention of buying them. "This was only for fun. That's what you said."

"And it'll be even more fun if they're yours."

"B-but," she stammered.

"Let me do this for you, Nicki," he said softly. "I *want* to."

He handed the woman his credit card to pay for the packages.

Before they left the mall, Sean had bought himself two new polo shirts. Sona had a new outfit and a new stuffed Dalmatian puppy that she refused to put in a sack. Even now, she carried the cute animal tucked up under her little arm. And besides the four new outfits, Nicki also carried from the mall a new pair of dress shoes.

"They're ridiculously flimsy," she told him when he'd insisted on the purchase. "They'll never hold up in the mountainous winter."

Sean only shrugged. "But they make you feel good, right?" And they had both broken out in laughter.

They climbed into Sean's car, buckled up their seat belts, and he said, "How about some dinner? I'm sure Sona must be starved." He looked at Nicki. "So what will it be? Indian? Italian? French? This city has anything you could want."

He pulled into traffic, and Nicki watched him. Should she ask? she wondered. Would he be upset with her when she told him what she'd *really* like to eat?

"Well," she hesitantly began, "if you really want to know..."

Sean glanced at her. "I really do," he said.

Still, she hesitated. Finally, she blurted, "I'd like a cheesesteak sandwich."

"*A cheesesteak?*" He looked incredulous.

Her brow wrinkled in an apologetic expression and she nodded slowly. "That is what Philly's famous for, isn't it?"

His mouth quirked up. "Yeah, I guess you're right."

Nicki whooped. "I've never had one before."

He took one look at the joy on her face and broke out in laughter. "Okay," he said. "Let's get the lady the cheesesteak she wants."

After the last morsel of sandwich had been devoured, the last potato chip had been eaten, Sean said, "Well, now I guess everyone can go home happy."

Nodding, Nicki told him, "Well, I'm a lady with new clothes, new shoes, and belly full of delicious, greasy food." Leaning back, she pressed her palm to her belly. "I really don't think I'm in Philadelphia at all."

He balled up the paper wrappers, tossing them onto the tray. "And where is it you think you are?" he asked Nicki, humor feathering the corners of his mouth.

She swiped her lips with the napkin one last time, and whispered, "Heaven."

He shook his head ruefully. "You are just too easy to please. That's all there is to it."

Nicki felt good. Happy and content. She and Sean and Sona had spent a wonderful afternoon together, shopping, eating, laughing. As they drove toward home, she couldn't help but feel that now would be the perfect time to talk to Sean about her observations. Tell him what was on her mind.

She really thought he needed to find himself a wife. A good woman who could help him make a home for Sona. Someone he could share his life with. Someone to share his burdens and responsibilities.

When the idea had first come to her, she simply hadn't thought she knew him well enough to be giving him advice. But a whole week had gone by. A week during which they had spent lots of time together. And after their lovely day, maybe he would be open to a little friendly counsel.

Turning her head, she checked on Sona who was happily chewing on the ear of her new stuffed puppy. Then Nicki looked at Sean's handsome profile, held her breath for the fraction of a second that it took for her to formulate how to broach the topic. No better way, she decided, than to simply come right out with it.

Then she blurted, "You know what you need?" Without giving him a single moment to respond, she dramatically proclaimed, "*A wife.*"

Chapter Six

"**W**hat?" he said.

She had to admit, he looked truly perplexed. He had obviously heard her clearly, but it seemed he had no clue why she'd make such an outlandish suggestion.

"Well, um..." She suddenly felt a little less sure of herself and the advice she was about to offer. Finally, she stammered, "A... a wife. You know. A real wife. A woman who—"

His bewilderment seemed to instantly dissolve. "I have a wife, thank you."

His tone held a pleasant, joking quality. Then she noted that his mouth curled up at the corners. A thought came to her; he thought she was teasing him.

"I'm serious, Sean."

He glanced at her, confusion and wariness easing back into his dark eyes. Then he quickly directed his gaze back out at the roadway ahead.

"You lead an awfully solitary life," she continued. "It would be good for you—and for Sona—if you had someone. You know, to share things with. I mean, I'm here now. And we have a great time laughing at the mischief Sona gets herself into." Nicki looked out at the horizon, thinking of their week together. "That face she made when she stole the lemon wedge from your glass of water and tasted it. Or when she got herself stuck under the living room chair like a cork in a bottle. Or like the few moments this week she scared us to death when we couldn't find her. And all the time she was sitting in your closet, playing with your shoes."

Even now, Sean chuckled easily. "She had lined them all up. She was making a train."

"And when she first met Chunky," Nicki reminded him. "She squealed with glee and went toddling after that cat as fast as her tiny legs would carry her."

"And Chunky went running, too," Sean said.

"Poor thing didn't come out from under the porch for hours."

Nicki allowed a silence to fall between them. Then she said, "You're going to have a million of those kinds of things happen while Sona's growing up. You should have someone to share them with. It's been nice for me to be that someone, but I won't be here much longer." She felt the need to reiterate. "You'll need someone."

Sean didn't take his eyes off the highway as he lifted his shoulders in an unperturbed shrug. "I'll share those times with Sona."

That's not the same thing, she wanted to tell him. She wondered if he was purposefully missing her point.

"You're going to have some rough spots ahead of you," she pointed out. "When she's exposed to other children, she's sure to get the sniffles. And she's bound to come down with bouts of chest colds, and ear infections, once the weather turns chilly. You'll need someone's help. A real, stick-around wife would be the perfect solution."

The light laughter he emitted sounded slightly forced. "Believe me, Nicki, my daughter is the only female I need in my life."

Heck, she'd waded out into the swamp this far, she might as well dive into the deep end.

"I know you told me you were a confirmed bachelor," she began, "but I honestly didn't think you meant you intended to stay that way forever. But now I'm getting the feeling that you have no intention of *ever*... um... you know, getting involved."

He pulled onto the main street that wound through his neighborhood. "Why would you think anything else? I told you that was my intention when we first met."

Nicki gave a small shrug. "Well, yes. You did. But I kind of thought that might be because you just hadn't met the right woman or something."

His lips pursed, and he said nothing.

"However, over the past week I've heard you make... certain comments. Things that have led me to believe you really mean to stay single." She felt the muddy waters closing in around her, but she couldn't help but ask, "Were you hurt in the past?" Then she quickly said, "I mean, you don't have to tell me if you don't want to. But it's awful not to be able to trust. Not all women—"

"Wait," he said, turning the steering wheel and directing the car onto his long driveway.

But Nicki was on a roll. "—are evil," she plowed full steam ahead. "You need someone, Sean. You need a woman. Someone to be with. Someone who is willing to stay—"

"Are you vying for the position?"

This unexpected question had her spine straightening in surprise. She blinked several times. "Of course not. This isn't about me. How could you think that it is? I can't stay here. You know that. This is about *you*. And Sona. The two of you need someone to—"

"Stop."

The one small word was quiet but tight as a coiled spring, and it cut Nicki's sentence to the quick.

"You've got it all wrong," he told her. "I wasn't hurt in the past. No one trampled on my feelings. No one damaged my ego. No one wounded my pride." He brought the car to a stop, cut the engine, and got out of the driver's seat. He opened the back door and unlatched Sona from her car seat. It was clear to Nicki that he was simmering with anger.

With Sona on his hip, one of her arms curled around his neck, the other snuggling her new stuffed puppy, he bent at the waist just enough so that he could gaze steadily at Nicki who remained, stunned to stillness, in the front seat of the car.

"Despite what you might believe, there wasn't some evil woman in my past who destroyed my ability to place my confidence in others." He hoisted Sona into a more secure position in his arms. "I have no trust issues. Believe me. If I did, I wouldn't trust *you* with what has become the absolute treasure of my life."

Then he directed his attention at Sona. "Come on, sweetie. It's time for you to have a nice bath and get ready for bed."

He closed the door of the car and went toward the house, leaving Nicki sitting all alone in the total silence.

She watched him disappear into the house. She felt wounded, chagrined, and fully put in her place. All she had meant to do was offer a little friendly advice. Why had her amiable intentions gone so awry?

Let it go, a tiny voice warned from the very back part of her brain. *It's none of your business.*

So he had no trust issues. She nearly nodded when she remembered the confidence in his voice when he made the proclamation. He was telling the truth, she decided. And he'd given her ample proof. If he didn't trust her, he'd never in a million years have allowed her near Sona.

But why, then...

Let it go, the small voice repeated the command, this time more fiercely.

But Nicki only found herself becoming even more curious than she'd been before.

He'd confirmed his aversion to marriage and relationships. But if his antipathy hadn't been caused by a woman from his past... what *had* happened to bring about this adamant way of thinking? Why was he so tenaciously against marriage? Against loving relationships?

She sat in the silence of the car for a long while, pondering the curious questions flying around in her head like tiny, persistent gnats that simply refused to stop being an annoyance.

***

The feminine flowery scent that continuously wafted from Nicki filled Sean's office. It permeated the air, hovered around him, filled his lungs with each and every breath he took.

The two of them hadn't spoken more than

simple pleasantries ever since the evening she'd made that odd recommendation to him.

A wife. Nicki thought he needed a better half.

He realized she was only making the suggestion because she cared about him and Sona. Nicki wanted his little family to thrive once she flew off overseas to her next teaching position. After mulling over the conversation, he eventually understood that her motives were completely unselfish.

His angry, knee-jerk reaction had built up a wall between them. A wall that seemed to grow thicker each day.

He should apologize for snapping at her as he had. But he just couldn't bring himself to do that. Because then he'd be forced to explain his behavior. And that was simply something he couldn't imagine doing. He'd rather walk over red-hot coals barefoot than tell Nicki the truth about why he never intended to marry.

Darting a covert glance at where Nicki and Sona sat on the carpet, he clenched his jaw. Nicki was a beautiful woman. With her fiery hair trailing down her back, her jewel-green eyes so inquisitive and lively. Being in the same room with her was torture for him. That's not entirely true, he silently amended. Just thinking about her was torture for him. Her luscious curves, her womanly scent...

Stop! he commanded himself. This was insane. If he kept dwelling on these thoughts of her, he'd never conquer the urge to reach out to her, kiss her, touch her, *taste* her. He held his breath, suppressing a moan of sheer torment. This need was so damned vexing!

"Look, Sona," Nicki said softly. "Daddy's watching us draw."

Actually, it was Nicki who was doing the sketching, forming big, colorful shapes and then naming them in English for Sona.

The fact that she'd caught him watching her made him feel awkward.

"That's a circle, sweetie," she told Sona. "A big, green circle." Then Nicki looked up at him. "That's a hard word to form. *Circle.* But she'll be able to say it in English very soon."

There it was, he realized. The bright but forced friendliness that was like concrete and bricks. The wall they had erected to protect themselves. Nicki's gaze slid from his, telling him she recognized the barrier, too.

Damn it! He hated this tension. He stared,

unseeing, at his computer screen. But how could he ease it without being forced to reveal—

"Sean."

His gaze flew to Nicki's face. Something in her tone had him feeling wary. Her eyes held a hint of sadness.

"I know I told you I'd stay and help you for a couple of months, but maybe it would be best if..."

Her voice faltered, and she took a deep breath.

In a firm tone, she said, "Maybe it's time for me to go. You and Sona are getting on just fine."

And things between us are so awkward, he heard her silent message.

His whole body tensed. "You can't go yet."

"But..."

"The only reason things have gone so smoothly," he told her, "is because you've been here to interpret for me."

Nicki looked dubious. "You know most of what Sona says now. She asks for milk. Or cookies. Or tells you her diaper's wet. Elementary things. Things you'd figure out even if I wasn't here."

"You can't go yet," he repeated.

Why was he feeling so threatened by her suggestion to leave? His mind was whirling too quickly to come up with an answer.

Her voice quieted as she said, "The situation between you and Sona might be smooth and sweet as... as homemade vanilla pudding. But things between you and I..." She hesitated, pressed her lips together, and then began again. "I keep wondering when one of us is going to have the guts to admit that thunderclouds are hovering over us. Again."

Sean didn't want to discuss the moments right after their shopping excursion and their cheesesteak dinner a few days ago. He didn't want to have to explain his behavior, his anger. So he remained silent.

"Look," she told him, "it was never my intention to bring discord into your home. Don't think I haven't noticed how little work you've gotten done since I made that stupid suggestion to you the other night about your finding a wife."

She was obviously waiting for him to say something. He didn't. *Couldn't.*

"I should have kept my advice to myself," she said. "I know that now. And I'm sorry that I made you angry." She looked down at Sona and then back at him. "Living with this... stiff silence is silly. It's time for me to go. You can send the annulment papers to me. I can sign them—"

"The annulment." His eyes went wide.

After only a second's hesitation, she said, "What about it?" Then her head cocked to the side. "You have been working on it, haven't you?"

Oh, heavens. Sean actually groaned.

"Nicki, I forgot all about it."

"You forgot?" Her brow creased as she evidently wondered how such a thing could have happened.

"I'm sorry." He stood up, picked up his phone, and began scanning through the numbers. "I'll call my attorney. Today. I'll get the paperwork started. It can't take long to get the necessary forms filed." With his little black address book in hand, he headed for the door of his office. "You and Sona stay put. I'll talk in the kitchen."

For the life of him he couldn't understand his frantic reaction to her proposal to leave. Even though he knew she'd meant it as an offering—a peace offering, he was sure—he hadn't taken it that way at all. For some reason, he intuitively heard a… threat. And that's what had him feeling the need to escape his office, *her*. He didn't understand *why* he was feeling threatened; he only realized that he was.

At the door, he turned to face her, trying hard to calm his thoughts, get himself under control.

"About the trouble between us," he said. "We'll talk. Okay? We'll smooth things out. We'll make it better, Nicki. I promise. I don't want you to feel uncomfortable around me. But you can't leave me just yet. Not until Sona can communicate with me. I... I need you."

That was as much as he was able to admit before turning on his heel and escaping.

That night, Sean was unable to sleep so he went downstairs and snapped on the television. The news anchor's voice droned softly in the still room as his thoughts churned.

He'd been jumpy and preoccupied all evening. Sona had sensed his agitation and she'd ended up fussing and refusing to go to bed. In the end, she'd cried herself to sleep while he'd rocked and sung until his throat felt raw. That had been the first time that had happened since they had left Sona's home country. Nicki had hovered around the nursery door. She'd asked only once if there was anything she could do. He'd turned down her offer, feeling the need to handle the problem on his own. Finally, Nicki had gone into her room and shut the door. Sean had felt both relieved—and very much alone.

The problem was clear. He had to make things right with Nicki.

Their relationship was so darned volatile. Like a seesaw, they tilted back and forth. They had started out great. Then he'd made the mistake of kissing her. And no sooner had they gotten *that* situation worked out and explained away, when he'd become angry over her simple suggestion that he marry. Yep, he silently decided, their friendship was most definitely like a teetering playground seesaw.

Making peace with her was what he needed to do. But the difficulty would be in apologizing without explaining too much. To go into too much detail about his past would surely make him look bad in her eyes.

At that moment, she rounded the corner. Sean's breath caught in his throat. She looked like a vision in her simple white nightgown, the thin straps revealing her milky-white shoulders.

"I'm sorry," she said. "I didn't know you were down here."

"It's okay," he told her. Something in her gaze had him asking, "Are you okay?"

"I—I just had a bad dream." Reaching up, she combed her fingers through her long hair. Then she placed her palm at the base of her throat. "I thought I might have heard something outside."

Sean scooted to the edge of the couch. "I've been down here for a while. I haven't heard a thing." She still looked uneasy, and he stood up.

"Let me go outside and have a look around." The relief and gratitude reflected on her beautiful features made him feel ten feet tall.

The night was still and hot and quiet. He checked the perimeter of the house, the garage and then went into the barn. Both horses were breathing slow and steady, obviously asleep. The only excitement was when Chunky darted from the corner of the barn and curled around his legs looking for some attention.

Bending down on his haunches, Sean scratched the cat behind the ears. "You out hunting, girl?" he asked. Chunky meowed, her ears pricking up, and then she plunged back into the long shadows cast by the moon.

When Sean returned to the house, Nicki had obviously gone upstairs to fetch her robe. The delicate curves of her shoulders were no longer visible, but Sean knew that all he had to do to if he wanted to conjure them was to close his eyes.

Quickly pushing the thought from his mind, he

told her, "All's clear. Everything's quiet out there. Not a sign of trouble."

Appreciation shined in her sparkling green eyes. Sean looked away, forcing himself to breathe slowly.

"I made us some herb tea," she said, using a spoon to stir the hot liquid in one mug. "I hope you don't mind having some company for a little while. I sometimes have trouble sleeping. Not often. But sometimes." She gave a slight grimace, her voice softening. "Tonight seems to be one of those times."

The small apologetic smile she gave him made his heart lurch. The thoughts of her and the state of their friendship that had been keeping *him* awake were at the very forefront of his mind.

"Listen, Nicki," he said, easing himself down on the couch beside her, "I'm awfully sorry if... if the tension between us is upsetting you to the point that you're losing sleep."

He unwittingly rubbed his fingers across his forehead. "I've been thinking about... you and me. About how our... friendship has been so up and down ever since we met." He swallowed. "One minute we're having great fun together, the next minute I'm... biting your head off."

The memory of the words he'd tossed at her after their shopping trip made him flinch. He murmured, "I'm sorry about that, too." He rushed ahead. "I want us to get along. Sona and I are going to need you for weeks yet. I want you to be comfortable here. I want you to feel at home."

She laced her fingers around her mug of tea. "I won't lie to you. It does bother me to know that you're angry with me. I should never have tried to offer you unsolicited advice—"

"But I do understand why you did, Nicki," he quickly told her. "You had good intentions."

Her smile was small as smiles go, but seeing it did strange things to him. His blood seemed to heat up, the muscles low in his gut tightened. Reaching for his mug of tea, he turned his attention from her long enough to get a firm grip on the physical reactions of his body. However, the reactions were autonomic; there wasn't much a person could do to control rising blood pressure. Or runaway testosterone.

When he finally did look at her again, he firmly said, "I'm not angry, Nicki. Honest." Then he said, "And I'm sorry I snapped at you. I shouldn't have been so... curt."

Fully intending to let it go at that, Sean eased

back on the couch and stared at the television screen. He simply couldn't explain himself further. He couldn't afford to reveal his past to her. She'd never understand. Hell, he didn't understand how he could have done what he did. How could he expect Nicki to? So, he'd simply say nothing more about it.

The quiet grew ever more noticeable with each passing second. Darting a covert glance her way, he saw that she, too, was watching the TV. But there was something about her air, something about the tightness in her shoulders that revealed that she really wasn't as absorbed by the colorful car commercial playing on the screen as she pretended to be.

He felt an... expectation about her. As though she wanted to talk.

Sean could easily understand that, seeing how nervous she was when she'd first appeared in the living room. He decided it would be in her best interest if he were to engage her thoughts. Get her mind on something else. Make her forget, at least for a while, about the bad dream that had disturbed her.

"You know," he began, "I was raised in this house."

"Oh," she said, lifting her gaze to his, "that's nice. I know I've said this before, but it bears repeating. You do have a beautiful home."

He smiled and accepted her compliment with a small nod. "I was born right here in

Philadelphia. Went to grade school here. And college." After a moment's hesitation, he asked, "Where were you born? Where do you call home?"

His smile wavered when he saw her stiffen. She was quick to try to hide her reaction, but not quick enough.

"Well, I was born in Elkhart, Indiana," she told him. "But home is wherever I happen to be."

Was it his imagination, or did she place an extra bit of emphasis on her final statement?

"So you're a midwestern girl, huh?"

Nicki only smiled, then busied herself taking a sip of tea.

"What did your dad—"

"I don't have a dad."

She seemed just as surprised by her blurted statement as he was. Color flushed her cheeks with obvious embarrassment.

"Of course I had a father," she corrected. "What I meant to say was that I never knew him, never met him."

Her nervousness was apparent.

"Ah, so you were raised by your mother?"

Nicki's gaze slid from his. "No." The tiny word was barely discernable. "I was raised in foster homes."

"Oh," was all Sean could think of to say, and he'd been helpless to keep his surprise at bay.

Then the most peculiar thing happened. Nicki sat up straighter, fixed a bright smile on her face and allowed her usual happy-go-lucky persona to shine through.

"It wasn't a bad life," she told him. "In fact I'd say, all in all, I had a pretty good childhood. I learned to deal with all different kinds of people by living in all those homes. With all those—"

There was the shortest of hesitations here, but Sean couldn't help but notice it nonetheless.

"—families. I learned independence. I learned that I can count on myself. That I can be my own best friend." She nodded happily. "I learned I can survive. Just about anything."

The easygoing, upbeat rhetoric seemed somehow... *off*. Something wasn't right. Her positive show was just that. A show. Sean got the distinct impression that Nicki was desperately trying to cover something. And her efforts were nearly successful. Nearly.

He should back off. He knew that. If she wanted to hide behind a smile, then he should let her. But there was something about her eyes. A sad light that glistened in her green gaze. A poignant aura needing release. It touched Sean. Called out to him. And he felt he simply had to reach out. To answer.

"It really wasn't all that wonderful. Was it?"

For a moment, her features hardened into a fierce, protective mask, and he thought she had every intention of remaining hidden behind the shield of blithely optimistic energy she'd erected.

But then his gaze was drawn to a small movement of her creamy throat as it convulsed with a tense swallow. Her shoulders slumped, and the sigh she breathed overflowed with weariness.

Chapter Seven

The vulnerability radiating from her was nearly his undoing. He wanted to reach out to her. Touch her. Assure her. Let her know that, no matter what she might have endured, everything would be okay. That he'd make it so.

But he battled the overwhelming urge to make physical contact. He knew doing so wouldn't be appropriate. However, he intended to connect with her in other ways. With concern. Kindness. Caring. As much as he was able to, anyway. Because these were the things he sensed she needed now.

"You, um," she finally offered, "you're absolutely right."

Her voice sounded so young, so assailable.

When she swallowed and tucked her bottom lip between her teeth, his impulse to protect her increased tenfold.

"My childhood wasn't all that wonderful."

The tightness in her shoulders, the discomfort in her expression clearly conveyed to him that this hard-wrought admission went completely against the grain of her normal easygoing, affable nature. Sean recognized at that moment that she hid a great deal behind that gorgeous smile of hers and his curiosity kicked into high gear as he wondered what she had gone through during her adolescent years.

Her obvious uneasiness made his gut churn. He actually felt the need to grip the tea mug in both his hands to keep from touching her, soothing her, even though he didn't know yet what she was about to reveal.

"I went into foster care at such an early age," she continued, "I have no memories whatsoever of either of my parents."

Nicki was an orphan. Just like his little Sona. The revelation created a frown on his brow that bit deeply into his forehead.

Almost as if reading his thoughts, Nicki clarified, "I wasn't actually an orphan. Not in the strictest sense of the word, anyway." She looked away as if it were painful for her to admit. "I was abandoned."

Heaving a deep sigh, she continued, "I was shuffled from foster home to foster home. That's all I remember. Making new friends and having those friends ripped out of my life after a few months or a year. Sometimes a couple of years."

Her gaze shifted from the far corner of the room to the tea in her mug. "I did have some good experiences. Most of the adults who cared for me were kindhearted, generous people willing to open their homes to homeless kids. But some of the foster homes were run by people just looking to make a buck off the state. Taking in foster kids was a way to do it. And they'd make a profit by feeding us the most inexpensive food they could find, supplying us with faded and worn out second-hand clothing and shoes."

Sean watched as her eyes glazed over with the unpleasant past. He doubted that she was even aware that he was sitting next to her, so absorbed did she become in her story.

"I have to say, I was very lucky," she continued. "I was only in one abusive home. The foster parents were very strict. Disciplinarians, they called themselves. I guess I deserved the punishment I got." Her voice grew faint and far-off, and Sean knew she'd become totally lost in the past.

"I remember one spanking well," she whispered. "I hadn't made my bed. I knew it was an important rule. The law, really. You didn't come down to breakfast unless your bed was made. But I'd overslept and I would have gotten into trouble if I'd been late for school."

Her beautiful face scrunched up with the indecision she must have felt as a child. Which rule should she break? Not making the bed? Or being late for school?

Sean's heart split as he contemplated the rock-and-a-hard-place Nicki was describing herself stuck in.

"My third-grade teacher noticed the welt that the belt had left on my leg and she called Social Services." Her chin tipped up a fraction. "I was taken out of that foster home immediately."

"Good." Sean couldn't contain the blurted response. "I hope the state closed down the home."

She blinked twice, as though his voice jerked her back to the present.

"Oh, I'm sure that didn't happen," she was quick

to answer. "The need for foster parents was too great. Probably still *is* too great. Too many kids. Too few homes. I'm sure the people were warned, but—" she shrugged "—that probably changed nothing."

"But that's ridiculous!" He felt angry. Outraged. At the people who had hurt Nicki. At the state for allowing the treatment to continue on other innocent children.

But these things had happened to Nicki so long ago. His anger drained away until nothing was left but a nagging sadness.

"Something wonderful happened when I was in the seventh grade." Her face brightened considerably with a smile. "I had a teacher who played some Spanish tapes for the class. The next day, I came to school speaking some Spanish. Even putting some words together to make sentences. For some reason, the words and phrases just stuck in my head. Mr. Callahan was amazed. So was I, actually. He ended up working with me all year. We listened to French records and cassettes. And then Italian. Russian. All kinds of languages. It seemed very easy for me to pick them up. It felt like a game to me."

The wonder expressed on her face made her

more gorgeous than ever. Sean sucked in his breath, waiting for her to continue.

"I moved out of the school district," she said, "so I lost track of Mr. Callahan. But I never lost my love of languages. I studied French and Italian in high school. The counselor didn't want me to. She tried to tell me the classes would be too much. That one foreign language would be enough for me to handle. But I proved to her I could do it. And I continued to learn other languages on my own." She grinned. "I earned a full scholarship to state college."

Setting her tea mug down on the coffee table, she said, "Whoever gave me this wonderful gift—God, or Fate, or Mother Nature. The Universe..." She shook her head and shrugged. "It saved me. Gave me something to focus my energy on. It gave me direction. And a way out."

There was something hauntingly sad in her last statement, he thought, something that needed pondering. But he didn't take the time to think it through. His urge to respond was too great. He quietly said, "And now you use your gift to teach other kids."

She nodded, and went silent. But her mind was

still churning with the past. Sensing that she had more to say, he waited.

"I did try looking for my parents," she told him. He could see the sorrow and rejection she'd so very obviously experienced even before she spoke.

"When I was eighteen, I went to Child Services." Her jaw tensed. "What I discovered is that there's no known information about my father at all. Not a name or an address. Nothing. My mother listed my father's name on my birth certificate as John Doe. She gave me up to the state the day I was born. She'd signed a paper refusing to have information about herself released. To me. To anyone. Ever. The state's hands were tied. They couldn't tell me a thing. I tried searching social media. Facebook, Twitter, Instagram. But I couldn't find her."

She suppressed her anguish well. But Sean couldn't help but perceive it, be deeply affected by it. This woman needed to be held. Needed to be hugged. Needed some physical consolation.

Setting down his mug, he slid over and gathered her up in his arms. And there was not one nuance of hesitation in her as she allowed herself to be enfolded in his embrace.

"It's okay," he whispered against her sweet

smelling hair. "There's not a whole lot you can do about the choices two people made all those years ago. Who knows what kind of circumstances they were in? It could be that they were very young and unable to..."

He let the sentence trail, realizing that nothing he could say would lessen Nicki's pain. There were no words that could take away her feeling of rejection. No matter what situation he might explain, no matter what sympathetic picture he might try to paint to explain her parent's behavior. So he simply shut up and hugged Nicki to him, not really understanding what he hoped to accomplish. Maybe this close contact would somehow make up, just a little, for all the love and compassion she'd missed throughout her childhood.

Long minutes passed, and Nicki seemed content to take refuge in his arms. She didn't cry, but he could feel the sorrow fairly oozing from her. He rubbed his palms up and down her back in a slow, rhythmic motion.

Soon, Sean became aware of the softness of her skin beneath his fingertips, the warm, meadow-flower fragrance of her body so close to his, the feel of her firm breasts pressed against his chest.

This wasn't the time for him to feel aroused, but, heaven help him, that's exactly what he felt.

And this was no gentle, slow-growing germination of passion. Fiery desire reared its head seemingly out of nowhere. Rolling over him in a flash. Nearly crushing him, like a huge wall of water. One instant he was full of concern, the next he was brimming with a need so fierce it almost stole away his breath.

His blood pulsed thicker and hotter with each passing second. He wanted to tip back his head, to savor the sight of her pale-as-porcelain face, gaze into her gem-green eyes, kiss her rose-wine lips, until there was no trace of sadness left in her.

But he couldn't do that. This wasn't the time. Or the place.

Then he remembered that there wouldn't ever be a right time or place. Not with Nicki. She was too good, too fragile, for the likes of him. The few women he had chosen to date knew up front that he didn't intend to commit himself. He favored women who could take care of themselves. Who were just as... selfish and self-serving as he. That way, when he was ready to end a relationship, which he invariably did, he felt comfortable that the woman would be okay. That he wouldn't leave her feeling broken and floundering.

Nicki wasn't in that class. She was vulnerable. Loving. Caring. He'd end up hurting her for sure. So he had to rein in these physical feelings. He simply *had* to.

The flat of her palm pressed against his chest as she gently pushed herself away from him. Lifting her chin, she looked into his eyes. Sean thought he was going to melt under the heat of her gaze. She studied his lips, then raised her eyes to his once again.

Passion enveloped her, too. That fact shined as clear and bright as a beautiful spring morning.

The urge to kiss her hit him like a sucker punch to the gut. He all but doubled over from its force. But still, he refused to surrender. This woman meant too much to him. Meant too much to his little girl.

The soul-wrenching hunger reflected in Nicki's exquisite expression matched his own. They both wanted this moment to develop into... something more. Yet neither followed through on the need that was so obviously pulsing through them. Neither was willing to cross that line. To take that first step.

Nicki's motives for hesitating weren't completely clear to him. He had lots of pieces to the puzzle of who she was, how she thought, but he hadn't quite put them all together.

Sean, on the other hand, knew without a doubt why he didn't act. His reasons were sound. Strong. And right.

Finally, she swallowed, and pushed herself farther away from him. His arms slid from around her, his hands dropping to his sides.

"You're a good man," she whispered. "A very good man."

Gratitude tinged her tone, and it actually made him feel a bit chagrined about the deep desire throbbing in him, about the passion that continued to push him toward the edge of sanity. He didn't feel like a good man. The hunger pulsing through him had him feeling anything but.

"Thanks for letting me..."

Her shy hesitation was sweet.

"...lean on you."

Sean's exhalation was slow and even as he struggled to control all that he was feeling. There was just something about this woman that brought out the protector in him. The tough guy willing to take on the world.

"Anytime, Nicki," he told her softly. "You know that."

But she looked away as if she didn't... or as if she didn't want to. He stifled a groan. He hated to think that the awkwardness might creep up between them again.

As if sensing his thoughts, she said, "Enough of this miserable talk of the past. Tell me what you found out today. About the annulment."

Sean sighed, grateful to have a subject of conversation that was manageable, businesslike. This, he could handle.

"Well," he responded, "I found out that it'll be pretty easy. And pretty swift. My lawyer will start filing the papers tomorrow. And as long as both of us can state that there was no... um... ah... you know—" He suddenly stumbled over the words. "As long as there's no... physical relationship, no consummation, we'll be just fine."

Her flat-mouthed smile was her attempt to hide her embarrassment, but he couldn't help but notice how cute she looked with her cheeks tinted pink.

"We knew that, though, didn't we?" she asked, avoiding his eyes. "There hasn't been any trouble there."

He wondered how she could say that with what

they had both experienced just thirty seconds before. He'd certainly had trouble keeping his hands to himself. Oh, well, he decided, attesting to false facts might make the truth easier to ignore.

They spent a few more moments talking about the legal ins and outs of the annulment, and when the subject waned, Nicki said, "I really should say goodnight. It's getting late. You'd better get to bed too. The sun will be rising before you know it, and so will Sona."

"You're right," he told her. "I'll head upstairs in just a few minutes."

She took their mugs with her, offering to put them in the sink on her way through the kitchen.

The TV continued to drone softly in the quiet once Sean was all alone.

He felt exhausted. As if he'd fought some huge battle... and had won. He knew the struggle had been against himself. Against his own physical wants and desires. Against his growing passion for Nicki.

He was confident that he could fight the physical attraction he felt for her again, should the need arise. And he was fairly certain it would. Heck, if willpower alone wasn't enough, there was always a long, icy shower just waiting to be utilized.

However, he was a little more concerned with the other attraction for her that had begun to stir in him. She conjured emotions in him he really didn't want to feel... *couldn't afford* to feel and continue to remain detached and objective about their relationship.

Yes, a good, cold shower might take care of the physical attraction that plagued him. But what about the emotional attraction? What about the more tender yearnings in his gut, in his heart, that continued to linger long after the needs of his body had once again grown manageable?

***

An afternoon bubble bath. The very idea was decadent.

Nicki stretched out in the tub, water lapping at her toes, belly and breasts, frothy bubbles tickling every inch of exposed skin. She closed her eyes, indulging completely in the luxury of simply being lazy. She sighed contentedly, sinking deeper into the water, doubting that anyone but the most wealthy citizens of Kyrcznovia even owned a bath tub, let alone took long, lazy soaks. She knew *she* hadn't enjoyed such an extravagance since... she had to stop and think... wow, she couldn't even remember when.

With Sona napping and Sean busy on his computer, Nicki relaxed with a good book in a bubbly, wet paradise. She didn't think life could get more blissful than this.

Inevitably, Sean entered her thoughts. And suddenly, her brain was filled with memories of how he had held her last night. Closing her fingers around the airy bubbles, she remembered the feel of his hard chest under her palms, the deliciously warm scent of him as he'd hugged her close. She easily pictured the desire that had danced in his mahogany eyes. Lowering her lids, she felt her body respond to the need he conjured in her. Her skin tingled all over, her belly heated deep down inside.

Slowly, she ran her fingertips over her flat tummy and then up toward her breasts, imagining it was Sean's touch she was feeling. Her nipples budded. Her breath quickened. Oh, how she wanted him. And *he* wanted her. She had known it. Had seen it in his eyes, felt it in the tenseness of his body.

Her eyes flew open and she swallowed nervously as that odd dismay filled her like a hazy fog, making her feel heavy and afraid. Why did she always experience this awful—

The thump she heard had her eyes widening. What was that? A door slamming? A...

The sound of heavy footfalls on the steps had her sitting up in the tub with such force that water sloshed onto the floor.

"Sean?" she called. "What is it?"

Then Nicki heard Sona's ear-piercing cry.

Having lived in this house for more than two weeks, Nicki knew Sona had many different cries. The little girl would give a whiny cry if she wanted attention, an angry cry if she was frustrated. She'd whimper when she was tired, or tearfully complain if she was hungry. But this was clearly an expression of pain.

Hopping out of the tub, Nicki was heedless of the water and soapy bubbles dripping onto the floor as she snatched up a towel. She wrapped it around herself haphazardly and jerked open the door.

She barreled into Sona's room and saw Sean standing at the crib, his daughter in his arms.

"Oh, Sean!" Her voice was shaky with fear. "What happened?"

"She tried to climb out of her crib. I found her on the floor. Thank God she's not seriously hurt."

The guilt in his gaze was so thick, Nicki wanted to reach out to him. And that's exactly what she did. Placing one hand on his arm, the other against Sona's back, Nicki said, "There's no way you could have known this was going to happen."

"She could have broken her neck," he said. "I've got to lower the crib mattress. There's got to be a way to do it...."

"I'm sure there is," she told him, the heavy self-blame in his tone ripping at her heart like sharp claws. "But right now, we ought to get some ice on that bump on her noggin."

Nicki hoped the playful term would lighten the mood, but Sean refused to be consoled. In fact, she quickly discovered she'd only made him feel worse.

"Of course!" he said, hurrying toward the door. "How could I be so stupid? I should put a cold compress on her forehead."

They rushed down the stairs to the kitchen. Nicki felt terrible that in mentioning the ice she'd only made him feel worse.

"The floor is carpeted," she reminded him above Sona's cries. "She couldn't have fallen too hard."

With his free hand, Sean pulled open the freezer door.

"Here," Nicki said, "let me get that."

She placed several ice cubes in a plastic bag and then surrounded it with a soft, clean dish towel. It took them several moments to get Sona to allow them to apply the ice to the angry red bump on her head.

Sean pulled out a chair and sat with Sona on his knee. Nicki kneeled down beside them, trying to divert the child's attention from what her daddy was doing. Sona had stopped sobbing, but she continued to whine and fidget.

"Well, at least she doesn't seem to be in a lot of pain," Nicki pointed out to Sean.

"Yeah, but there's still fear in her eyes. That fall scared the wits out of her."

Nicki could only nod. "Daddy will fix your crib, sweetie," she crooned to Sona who had squirmed around to face her.

"I should have set the mattress to the lowest position when I put together the damned crib," he said. "If I had, this wouldn't have happened."

"Yes, but you'd have strained your back trying to get Sona in and out of bed," Nicki gently pointed out.

"Better that than having her fall and break her arm or something."

He felt terribly responsible for his daughter's accident, and Nicki felt awful about that.

"Sean—" she placed her hand on his knee "—you're not going to be able to keep Sona safe every moment of every day. You'll keep her as safe as you can, but it's inevitable... things like this are going to happen. Bruised knees, scraped palms, lumps and bumps."

Sean just studied her, worry darkening his eyes.

"I remember," she continued, "in one of the foster homes where I grew up, there had been a safety gate placed at the head of a flight of stairs. A little boy—he was about Sona's age, maybe a little older—managed to climb over the gate. He fell down the stairs." She looked off, remembering the awful scene. "He broke his nose. And he got an awful black eye. Blood from his nose was everywhere."

She sighed, shoved the memory aside, and looked up at Sean whose gaze had shifted and was directed at the floor.

"The house was full of people," she told him, "yet nobody saw that child climbing over the gate. Kids just have a way of getting into predicaments they shouldn't. They just have a way of finding trouble."

Still he remained silent. So did Sona.

Sean's utter stillness, his inability to respond, told Nicki just how upset he was with himself, how culpable he felt that his daughter had been hurt.

She rubbed small circles on his knee, patted it twice, then rubbed again as she softly said, "You can't beat yourself up about this. We'll fix the crib so she can't climb out. Everything's going to be okay." He still refused to look at her. "It really is," she assured him. "Honest."

At that moment, Sona reached out and scooped a small mound of bubbles that had been clinging to Nicki's bare shoulder. The little girl giggled when the delicate bubbles popped and disappeared from her fingertips.

Nicki's eyes went wide, remembering suddenly that she'd been bathing when she heard the commotion in Sona's room. She looked down the length of her towel-clad body. The soft terry fabric parted high on her thigh, exposing a wedge of her white flesh. When she looked up into Sean's face, she realized in that instant that he wasn't focused on the floor as he silently condemned himself—*he'd been giving her bare legs an intense and ogling stare.*

Nicki was mortified. She gasped and jerked herself upright, tugging and pulling in some vain attempt to get the towel to cover more of herself than was reasonably possible.

Sean was obviously just as embarrassed as she, his eyes going as wide as saucers as his gaze latched onto her face. However, the expression quickly melted away, and she could see him fighting hard to suppress the sudden, and evidently unexpected, merriment that began to dance in his luscious nut-brown eyes.

She should feel humiliated by his leering. She should feel angry. She should feel appalled. Shocked. Infuriated. She should be feeling anything except... except... *flattered.*

Nicki would not smile at the way his mouth was slowly drawing back on one side, teasing and sexy. She would not!

But no sooner had the thought entered her head when her own lips were being tugged at by the makings of a beguiling grin. But she shouldn't. *She just shouldn't.*

Suddenly overcome with the irrepressible seduction scene that had materialized seemingly out of the very air itself, Nicki opened her mouth to take in a quick breath.

Sean was flirting with her, she could see it in his hungry eyes, in the sensual set of his mouth. He *wanted* her. A thrill shot through her, and then that vague, bone-chilling fear followed closely on its heels.

"I—I was in the tub." The obvious truth came out sounding like a lame excuse. She knew it, heard it, as soon as the words left her mouth. "Wh-when I heard Sona fall, I—I was scared half to death. I d-didn't know what had happened." Why couldn't she speak five full words without stuttering? She didn't have a speech impediment, damn it. Clearing her throat she stammered, "I—I didn't stop to..." Sheer frustration made the thought fade into oblivion and she balled her hands into fists.

His brazen smile only widened further. "I can see that."

The rich, lazy sound of his timbre caused a shiver to course across every inch of her skin. She broke out in gooseflesh and she felt her nipples contract into nubs. His eyes traveling over her body were almost as tangible as a physical touch, and after the very erotic thoughts she'd had of him only moments before in the tub...

Her throat convulsed and she automatically crossed her arms over her chest. There was really no gracious way to do this and not allow him to become privy to the exact reaction she was trying to hide.

"I—I really should go upstairs," she said. "I should—"

"Yes." He nodded, his now full, lopsided grin helplessly expanding with each millisecond that passed. "You *really* should."

She turned and darted from the kitchen, his delighted laughter ringing in her ears.

Chapter Eight

Sean was thoroughly enjoying the change in his relationship with Nicki. And he knew the bubbles-and-terry-cloth incident—which was how he'd dubbed the situation when Nicki had come running out of her bath a couple of days ago clad only in a few well-placed bubbles and a too short terry towel—had been the turning point.

They were playful with one another. Friendly and flirtatious. It was refreshing and fun, and Sean refused to even consider, let alone contemplate, all the implications of the change. He only focused, for the time being, on relishing it.

He checked the saddle on Blaze, and then did the same on Pepper. Nicki was dressing Sona, and then the three of them planned to ride into the park and share a picnic breakfast. These kinds of spur-of-the-moment happenings were the very reason he felt so blessed that he owned his own business and worked out of his home. When most men and women were fighting traffic on the Blue Route, he was sipping his coffee, enjoying the morning, or exercising one or the other of his horses in the parkland surrounding his home. Yes, he was truly blessed.

Sean realized that Nicki, too, was a blessing in his life. If she hadn't happened into that hotel restaurant in Kyrcznovia looking for a job, he wouldn't have custody of Sona right now. He owed Nicki a lot for all this happiness he was experiencing. And after hearing about her background, about her childhood, Sean only felt more protective of her—more *attracted* to her—than ever. The urge to offer her a little joy while she was in America seemed to drown out all the doubts and qualms and hesitations he'd felt up to this point.

Sure, the fact that neither of them were looking for long-term involvement, or romantic entanglements, was still in his mind. But that didn't mean that he and Nicki couldn't have some good times together with Sona. That they couldn't make some pleasant memories together. Some happy reflections she could cherish after she was gone. Just as he would.

After she was gone...

The words echoed in his head. His arms relaxed at his sides and his gaze lowered to study the straw under his feet. The concept of his house vacant of Nicki made him feel—

"We're ready!"

Nicki's bright-and-cheery voice jarred him out of his somber contemplation. Sona squealed a delighted greeting to Sean and then automatically reached out, straining to touch Blaze's nose.

"You do love these horses, don't you, pumpkin?" Sean gently pushed Sona's dark hair back from her face.

"Are you sure the harness is going to work?" Nicki asked him.

He nodded, knowing she was speaking of the backpack-type child seat he'd bought so he could take Sona out on the horse. "Everything will be fine," he assured her. "We'll take it nice and slow. Get her used to riding Blaze. And get me used to carrying her on horseback."

Nicki's concern charmed him. Heck, he'd found

there was little about her that he didn't find captivating.

When she didn't respond right away, he grinned at her and teased, "Are you doubting me?"

"Oh, no," she said. Then she chuckled. "If anyone can handle riding a horse while carrying a baby on his back, it's you." Then Nicki looked at his daughter, "Isn't that right, Sona? We have plenty of faith in your daddy. There's not much he can't handle."

Her praise made his chest swell. However, he couldn't help but wonder if her too bright tone meant that a shadow of worry might continue to cloud the confidence she espoused.

Crooking his index finger under Nicki's chin, he tipped up her face until she was forced to look him in the eye. "Everything will be fine," he promised softly.

The cool morning air crackled and snapped with electricity. Finally, she smiled demurely and said, "I have faith in you."

That soft-and-sunny smile did potent things to his libido. Sean thought his heart was going to thump right out of his chest cavity. Lord, but she was lovely.

He shrugged the straps of the harness over his

shoulders and then Nicki secured Sona into the canvas contraption. All the while, the child clapped and giggled, knowing something exciting was about to take place.

Blaze and Pepper were led out into the sunshine of the paddock, and Nicki asked Sean, "Everything's packed?"

"Yes."

With Sona strapped to his back, he wasn't much help to Nicki as she mounted Pepper, but he placed a steadying hand on her thigh once she got her leg over the saddle. Firm, warm flesh beneath his fingers. Liquid fire shot straight up his arm.

"Bagels and juice and fruit. All packed in your saddlebags." He was utterly amazed that he was able to respond in such a normal manner.

"I'm a beginner at this riding stuff, myself," Nicki reminded him, patting his hand where it rested on her leg.

With the heat of her thigh beneath his hand and the softness of her warm palm above it, he was sure his entire body would burst into flame at any moment. Spontaneous combustion. He slid his hand free and took a backward step.

He grinned as he gathered Blaze's reins in his hand, hoping to cover the chaotic physical response to her nearness. "I'll remember that I have two amateurs with me this morning."

They experienced one hair-raising moment when Sona cried out in fear as Sean hoisted himself up into the saddle. But once they were settled and he'd murmured some assurances to his daughter, she quieted, her tiny hands gripping her daddy's shoulders.

The trails were dappled with sunlight and colorful flowers sprouted here and there among the lush, green underbrush. Oak trees and evergreens towered above them, offering them cool shade from the summer heat.

After a twenty-minute ride during which they had met only a solitary jogger on the wide-open paths of the park, Sean suggested, "How 'bout we stop here and eat?"

"Sounds good," Nicki told him. Making the dismount look as sweet as a slice of apple pie, she hopped to the ground and looped Pepper's reins over a low-hanging branch.

Meaning to warn Sona that they were about to dismount, Sean said, "We're getting down, sweetheart." Without waiting for Nicki to translate his words, he swung his leg over the saddle.

Pain shot through his head and he squished his eyes shut, grimacing.

"Whoa," he cried out, reaching up and gently encircling his daughter's little wrists.

Nicki clapped a quelling hand over her mouth, but not in time to hold back her impulsive laughter. Ignoring the subsiding pain, he cocked his head and fixed her with a glare that had her trying even more valiantly to suppress her humor.

"Well," she finally said, "I think Sona found the perfect safety handles."

"Those are not handles," he said, gritting his teeth as he extricated himself from his daughter's death grip. "They're my *ears*."

Amusement evidently got the best of Nicki and she broke out in bubbling laughter. She kept trying to hold it off, but little by little it got the best of her. Sona joined in, seemingly quite delighted that she'd caused such a stir in the adults.

"Would you please help get this little urchin off my back?" he asked.

Nicki continued to chortle intermittently as she unfastened Sona's restraining belt and pulled the child free. All Sean could do was rub his flaming ears.

Sona toddled off toward the picnic table,

stopping along the way to investigate pinecones and pebbles and whatever else she could find on the ground. Sean tried to wiggle out of the harness, but one strap caught on his shoulder. Without being asked, Nicki came to his rescue. She peeled the canvas harness off his back and tossed it over his horse's saddle.

Planting his hands on his waist, he arched his back, stretching the muscles. He bent his neck one way then the other, working out the strain and kinks. Sensing Nicki slipping up behind him, he stilled when he felt the warmth of her palms slide over his tense shoulder muscles.

She kneaded his neck and upper back, digging her thumbs in at just the right places. He was able to stifle the groan of gratification that welled in his throat, but he did allow his eyelids to ease shut. Nicki had magic fingers. However, her gentle touch alone—without any rubbing or massaging—would have made him dizzy with pleasure. *Sensual* pleasure.

Then he felt her feather light fingertips gently tracing the outer rim of his left ear. His throat went dry and he stopped breathing, waiting.

"The redness is going away," she whispered. Her

tone turned light and deliciously teasing as she added. "I do believe you're going to live."

Her voice was close behind him, and it sent a luscious chill raking down every single vertebra of his spine. Wisps of fire flickered deep in his belly, licking at him, rousing a heated passion within him. He wanted to hold her close. Inhale the scent of her hair and skin. Touch the full length of her elegant neck with his fingers, with his lips. And in that one insane instant, he surrendered to the urges that tormented him.

With no warning, he turned, smiling at the surprise that registered on her lovely face, grasping her upper arms so she couldn't step away from him. Her emerald eyes went wide, and the desire flaring inside him forced his smile to wane.

"The morning sunlight turns your hair to copper flames," he murmured, sure that the metaphor was provoked by the profound fire burning in him—the fire that blazed hotter with each passing second.

Sean pulled her up against his chest, barely touched his nose to her temple. "And you smell wonderful."

She felt small in his arms. Delicate. And quivery. Like a fragile flower bud. Coaxing that bud to open to him suddenly seemed the most important goal on this earth.

He ran the tip of his nose down along her face, from temple to jaw line and then back up, daring to stroke her cheekbone with first the feathery touch of his chin, and then the light press of his lips. Her skin was as smooth and as pale as polished alabaster.

Inhaling deeply, fully, he was content at this moment to simply be near her. However, that contentment diminished swiftly, and he felt a terrible need to taste her, to touch her.

Sliding his fingers up behind her ear and into her silky tresses, he studied her eyes, wanting to gauge her reaction to what was happening between them. Wanting to gauge her reaction *to him.*

His newly formed daddy instinct had him darting a quick glance at his daughter, who was busying herself gathering a pile of pinecones and acorns, sticks and small rocks, so Sean felt safe focusing his attention once more on Nicki, assessing her response, discovering exactly what it was she was feeling.

Her expression was unreadable at first. Filled with a dark and thrilling mystery he wanted desperately to solve. Then he deciphered multilayers of complex emotion.

Uncertainty. Confusion. Wonder. Astonishment. Doubt. Was that a touch of fear? he wondered.

Then he saw it. Desire. Rich, heady and deep.

The passion he read in her gaze wavered, seemed to teeter on the very edge of her consciousness, as if she wasn't sure she should—or even *wanted* to—feel it. But it was there in her eyes, in her shallow breath, in her trembling body.

As if to confirm his thoughts, she softly whispered, "We shouldn't, Sean. We really shouldn't."

When she spoke the word *shouldn't*, her luscious lips puckered oh-so-slightly and he felt that if he didn't kiss her—then and there—that he'd surely shrivel into nothingness and disappear completely.

"I don't give a damn," he said, the overwhelming passion turning his tone to a growl. Staring deeply into her eyes, he asked, "Do you?"

The need pulsing through her evidently matched his own for, without hesitation, she shook her head back and forth once, twice, and then she relaxed into his arms.

She tasted faintly sweet, like warm mint, and

Sean savored the pleasant flavor of her. Her mouth was soft and pliant and hot, the taste and feel and scent of her making his body grow feverish.

Breaking away from him, she whispered against his mouth, "Sona."

Her concern for his little girl—right in the midst of their all-consuming passion—made him want to only hug her harder, kiss her more. Nicki was a marvelous human being. Caring, nurturing. Sexy as hell.

"She's fine," he assured her, casting another quick look at Sona to be sure he was telling the truth. His sweet angel baby was focused on separating the items she'd collected into piles. He looked at Nicki, who had closed her eyes, seemingly enjoying this forbidden caress just as much as he.

Maybe he should allow sanity a foothold in his brain. Maybe he should release her and embark on the impossible task of forgetting that this kiss ever happened. However, the need to hold her, to kiss her, had plagued him for *so very long*. For the first time in weeks, he felt his agony subside... all because holding her in his arms was having his craving satiated. So he just couldn't bring himself to give up this precious moment by setting her free just yet. He kissed one delicate eyelid. And then the other. One corner of her mouth. And then the other.

She opened her eyes, and for a single instant, Sean felt as if their very souls connected. It was then that he knew.

He was falling in love.

***

Dr. Smyth listened to Sona's heart and then pressed the stethoscope to her back. The pediatrician smiled at Sean when Sona squirmed and giggled.

"She sure is a happy child," the doctor commented.

Sean only nodded nervously. He wasn't going to allow the good doctor to distract him. He'd heard about infant immunizations, and he wasn't looking forward to the ones that were surely in his daughter's imminent future.

"A lot of toddlers usually scream bloody murder during their first visit to my office." The doctor set Sona on the scale and leaned over to fiddle with the weights until an accurate reading registered.

Sean's palms felt clammy and he unwittingly

rubbed them down the length of his khaki-covered thighs. He didn't like the idea that Dr. Smyth was going to hurt his little girl with needles, even though he realized that the tiny bit of pain was necessary and just might save Sona's life in the years to come. Still, he couldn't help feeling reluctant.

"Hmmm," the doctor murmured. "Her weight is on the low end of the spectrum."

Sean's ears pricked up. "Is that bad?"

"Well, she looks healthy enough."

"She's very healthy," he rushed to say. "As far as I know."

Dr. Smyth nodded, not taking her attention off Sean's daughter. The woman held up a ball and seemed pleased when Sona reached for it.

"Her sight and coordination seem normal," the doctor observed. "My guess is she didn't get a whole lot to eat during her time in the orphanage." She glanced at Sean. "How's her appetite been since you brought her home?"

"She eats like a horse."

The doctor smiled. "Good. I'll just make a note on her chart that will remind us to keep a close eye on her weight."

The examination continued for several

moments, and Sean's mind was once again nagged by the idea of those needles that he knew loomed in the very close future... like in the next five to ten minutes.

Placing Sona on the floor, the doctor encouraged the child to walk around the tiny room. "Her balance is great. She walks well. Like any other toddler her age."

Finally, Sean could hold in his anxiety no longer. "Let's talk about Sona's inoculations."

Dr. Smyth seemed taken aback by the abruptness and Sean felt heat suffuse his face.

"Okay," the pediatrician answered. "We can talk about her baby shots now, if you like."

Even though he tried to relax, he felt his muscles tense, his jaw tighten.

The doctor studied Sona's chart. Then she said, "As you know, your daughter received some of the necessary inoculations and her tuberculosis skin test before she was allowed to enter the country. However, there are a few she still needs to get started on."

"Started on?" He didn't like the sound of that.

Dr. Smyth nodded. "Immunizations are given in doses. Some of them take three doses. Some take four. And they're given over a span of time."

A frown bit into his brow at the prospect of having to suffer through this anxiety on pretty much an ongoing basis for the next year and a half.

Evidently the good doctor noticed his nervous apprehension. "I promise, Mr. Hudson—" she hesitated long enough to grin at him "—I won't prick *you* even once with a needle."

He smiled at her attempt to allay his apprehension, but the thought of seeing Sona cry still shadowed his thoughts.

"You know," Dr. Smyth continued, "maybe your wife should be in here with you and your daughter...."

"Oh, no—" his head shook back and forth quickly "—Nicki... the lady in the waiting

room. She isn't my wife. She's, um, our nanny."

The *our* sounded kind of silly, he thought as soon as the plural possessive had tumbled off his tongue. But that's how he'd thought of Nicki from the first day he'd met her. In a way that was quite personal. Special. So he really didn't care how it sounded.

"Ah, I see... well," the doctor said, obviously intent on making a second try. "Maybe you'd like for her to join us, anyway. You know, as a kind of moral support. For both you and your daughter."

The suggestion caused his whole body to react. He grew calmer immediately, and after moistening his lips, he sighed.

"You know," he said, "I think that would be a great idea."

Even though the doctor wielded the syringe with swift expertise, Sona still cried. Nicki and Sean both did what they could to comfort her as the doctor, completely unruffled by the tears, took a moment to jot down her final notes in the file.

"You did a great job, Sona," Dr. Smyth said, smoothing a loving hand down the child's arm.

But Sona only hid her face in the crook of her daddy's neck.

"Mr. Hudson, my secretary will set you up for your next appointment in two months."

Once the doctor left the three of them alone, Nicki immediately reached for Sona's clothing.

"Oh, Lord," Sean helplessly murmured. "I hate the idea of coming back here. No wonder children scream bloody murder."

"Scream bloody murder?" Nicki asked as she slipped a sock onto Sona's little foot.

"It was something the doctor said before you came in," he told her. "That her patients scream bloody murder. What I find amazing is that the parents of her patients don't scream. And kick. And run for their lives."

Nicki chuckled. "When Dr. Smyth came toward Sona with that needle, I thought for sure you were going to do just that." She quickly sobered. "It's necessary, you know."

He nodded, resignedly. "I do know." He cradled the back of his daughter's head with the palm of his hand. "It's just that... I thought my job was pretty clearly mapped out. To protect Sona from harm."

"And you're doing that," Nicki told him gently. "By bringing her here."

Again, he nodded. "But I feel so awful. So guilty."

Nicki roused Sona from Sean's protective embrace long enough to tug the child's dress over her little head. Then Nicki fastened the button at the back.

"I have to admit," Nicki said. "I thought my heart was going to break when I saw Sona begin to cry. But Dr. Smyth did her best to be quick."

He looked at Nicki and felt a rush of relief that she was here to share this miserable experience with him.

The three of them went out into the reception area and Nicki took Sona from Sean so he could pay for the office visit. Waiting at the counter for his credit card, he became acutely aware of Nicki standing by his elbow as she gently rocked Sona back and forth.

Since discovering his deep feelings for Nicki, he'd felt torn. On one hand, he wanted to tell her. He wanted to see if she might be willing to make a go at a real relationship with him. But on the other hand... he knew he should keep his mouth shut.

Was he willing to see her hurt? Because if he was to become involved with Nicki, that was the sure outcome. Pain and distress for her.

Who was he kidding? he silently asked himself. "The other hand" was the only hand—the only *choice*—he had. He simply must keep his mouth shut.

The receptionist promised to email Sean the receipt, and then they scheduled the date of Sona's next visit. He murmured a farewell, and turned to Nicki. His breath caught as he looked into her clear, beautiful eyes.

And he wondered how on earth he was going to be able to keep silent about what was in his heart.

Chapter Nine

"Hi, Bob," Nicki called out as she entered the barn.

As usual, the reserved caretaker nodded a silent greeting and then continued his task of spreading fresh hay in Blaze's stall.

The elderly man did his job, and did it well, without an abundance of conversation. Heck, without practically any conversation. Bob Davis was definitely a man of few words. And that's why Nicki felt safe coming into the barn to do the thinking she needed to do.

"Would you mind if I help you with the grooming today?" she asked the caretaker.

"That'd be fine," he said, casting her only a cursory glance.

Pepper's stall smelled of sweet, fresh hay. Nicki greeted the animal with a soft hello as she smoothed her palm down the length of the animal's neck. The grooming brush felt a bit heavy in her hand, but Nicki quickly got used to the weight of it as she ran the bristles over the horse.

The two weeks that had passed since she and Sean had shared that soul-shattering kiss in the park had been the most wonderful of her life. She knew in her heart that the flirtatiousness between them didn't—no, *couldn't*—mean anything. Sean had told her early on, when she'd suggested he find himself a real wife, that he simply wasn't interested in a relationship. And even if he was, Nicki knew she wouldn't be staying here much longer. In fact, she'd received an email that there was a teaching position for her in Slovakia. Seems she was needed immediately, but the job would be held for her for two weeks. She'd come out to the barn to plan the best way to break the news to Sean.

Another week here with him and Sona should be sufficient, she surmised. Then she could fly to Slovakia with time to spare, time to find a place to live and get her bearings in the new town, before starting the job.

With each day that passed, Sean seemed more

and more comfortable in his new role as Sona's daddy. And the toddler was obviously happy in her new home here in America. Before too much longer, neither one of them would need Nicki. However, that had been the whole idea from the beginning.

So, this flirtation she and Sean had been enjoying would soon be coming to an end. It might only have been temporary, but it sure had been fun! She hadn't ever—in her whole life—felt such delight, such pure, playful joy as she'd felt when she'd participated in their impish banter or when she'd been in Sean's arms or felt his mouth pressed against her own.

Pepper nickered softly, seeming to sense the lightheartedness that had Nicki's mouth curling into a whispery smile.

However, a small, dark cloud gathered over her when she thought about telling Sean about the job that was waiting for her halfway around the world. Surely, he'd be happy for her. Surely, he'd accept the news with—

Bob gave a soft cough and said, "I, ah..." Pleasantly surprised by the caretaker's obvious intention to talk with her, Nicki looked his way, her hand resting on Pepper's silky back.

"I've been meaning to tell you," he continued. "I don't ever think I've seen Sean so happy. He's usually stuck in that office of his twelve or fourteen hours a day. And now he's taking picnics out in the park, going shopping, talking, and laughing. It's really great. I've never heard him laugh so much."

Nicki blinked, once, twice. This was the most she'd heard Bob speak since meeting him weeks ago.

"He *is* happy," Nicki agreed. "Sona has really changed his life."

The elderly caretaker cleared his throat. "If you don't mind my saying so, I tend to think little Sona isn't the only reason behind his good spirits." Embarrassment warmed her cheeks. He was evidently hinting that she was behind the change in Sean. She felt the need to stop this before it even started. The man needed to be told the truth. She couldn't stay here.

Why not? The tiny question echoed in her head.

But she shoved it aside just the way she did every other time it had plagued her.

Slipping her palm from under the leather strap, she set the grooming brush aside and moved to the chin-high wall at the front end of the stall.

"You know, Bob," she said, "I'm not going to be staying here. I have a job to go to in Slovakia. I'll be leaving soon. I only came here to make Sona's transition go a little smoother."

Bob stopped spreading the hay and planted the rake on the barn floor. He gazed up at her for the first time. "Sean did tell me that. But it's just that..." His words seemed to falter. "Well, it just seems to me that...things have changed."

The saucy fun she and Sean had been having with one another might have been entirely innocent in their minds, but it was obvious that their behavior toward one another had been noticed by Bob, and it had altered the caretaker's perception of the situation.

When she didn't respond, he said, "Now I don't mean to be forward, and I probably shouldn't be sticking my nose into your business, but—" his shoulder lifted slightly in a small shrug "—having a woman in his life has been good for Sean. I'm afraid he might not tell you that. So I'm taking it upon myself to let you know."

Her lips eased back into a smile. Yes, he was being a bit forward, but she couldn't fault him for speaking out of concern for Sean. And it was so very clear that that was his motive.

Besides, Bob's observation that having a woman in his life was good for Sean only solidified in her mind the idea that Sona's daddy really did need a soulmate. Nicki had thought that from the very beginning. Granted, Sean hadn't liked the idea much when she'd brought it up, but that didn't make it any less true. He did need a woman in his life.

Nicki's mind churned. Maybe... just maybe... she could get up enough nerve to mention the notion to him again before she left his home for good. But this time, she'd have to plan an argument good enough to convince him.

"You haven't seemed all that unhappy here, yourself," Bob commented, a rare and wry grin splitting his wrinkled face.

"Oh, you're right there," she quickly assured him.

He seemed to be waiting for her to elaborate, and when she didn't, he said, "So, why do you have to be rushing off? When you and Sean seem to... you know, get along so well together."

His last statement contained more innuendo than Nicki was comfortable with. Again she felt embarrassed. She and Sean had been toying with one another. Playing with the physical attraction they both felt. But it didn't mean anything. It couldn't. It was just... fun. A dalliance. That was all. Yet, explaining all that to the caretaker just seemed too personal. Too intimate. Still, Nicki felt the man deserved to know the honest-to-goodness bottom line.

She unlatched the gate, stepped out of the stall, and then fastened the latch behind her. Then she went to the opening of the stall where Bob was standing. She needed to get closer. To make him understand, once and for all, how things stood.

"I can't stay here," she said, her voice sounding tiny and weak when she'd meant for it to come out strong and firm. She heard something else in her tone, too. Something she couldn't quite identify.

Bob chuckled softly. "You seem awfully uncertain about that."

That's what it was! Uncertainty. The fact that the caretaker had recognized the doubt in her tone when she herself hadn't, made her face flame.

"Tell me, Nicki," he said, "why can't you stay? It's a real nice place, this farm. And Sean's a good man. And that baby girl loves you to pieces."

"W-well... I-I," she stammered. She stopped, forced herself to take a deep breath in an effort to gather her wits that felt strewn about like so many stalks of straw. However, actually hearing the question—the same one that had tormented her, the same one that she kept pushing aside—really alarmed her to no end.

Then she blurted, "I have a job. In Slovakia."

Bob waved that notion off with a toss of his large, callused hand. "Aw, now. Jobs are a dime a dozen. You can work anywhere."

The fact that he was able to cast aside her one, good and solid excuse caused her more upset than she was able to bear. That strange, shadowy fear crept up on her and she panicked.

"I—I just can't stay here," she cried. And then she bolted from the barn.

***

"Well, it's nearly over."

The sound of Sean's voice nudged Nicki from her cozy, sluggish state. She sat in the dark in the screened-in back porch, just listening to the quiet sounds of the night. Sona had been tucked into bed, and Nicki had slipped into her satin nightgown and matching robe and had come out here to relax.

She knew she had plenty of problems to work

out. The way she'd literally scrambled to escape Bob and his questions in the barn yesterday. The nagging fear that refused to release its hold on her. The fact that she needed to tell Sean about the job she'd been offered. The idea that she really needed to stop this pointless teasing and flirting with him.

But she didn't want to stop! Sean made her feel so... pretty, so... happy, so... *alive*.

The porch had seemed like the perfect place to retreat with all these troubling thoughts. One thing was certain; since coming to America she'd become a master at evading anxiety and problems.

She sighed at the thought, grinning in the dark.

"What's nearly over?" she asked, tucking her feet up underneath her to make room on the wicker settee for him.

He sat down. "Our marriage."

"The annulment papers have arrived?" She sat up straight, placing her bare feet on the floor.

"Mm-hm," he answered, lifting the large manila envelope for her to see. "All we need to do is read and sign the documents, and then my lawyer will file them. And it's over."

"Wow." Nicki didn't know how she should feel.

Soon, there would be nothing left to hold her here.

Knowing of no other words to utter, she said, "That sure was fast."

"Damn legal system drags its feet with everything else," he muttered. "But with this it's swift, clean, and sweet." He gazed out into the darkness. "Just my luck."

"What do you mean?" The question pitched forth before she even had time to think. "This is what you wanted." She quickly amended, "What we wanted."

She saw him smile in the shadows, his teeth flashing in the dark.

"Of course," he assured her.

His grin tipped up farther on one corner, the charm of it making her heart flutter like the wings of a dozen butterflies.

"I was only teasing."

His voice had grown deliciously soft, and Nicki felt her blood heat. She should control herself. She had things she needed to discuss with him. The job that would take her away. And now the annulment papers.

The tips of her fingers feathered, back and forth, across the indentation at the base of her throat. "So," she said, the word coming out sandpaper rough, "what do we do now?"

He shrugged. "Nothing. Well, other than signing on the dotted line and mailing in these forms." Another dazzling smile. "Seeing as the annulment is uncontested, and there was no sexual contact, and no settlement to arrange."

The air went utterly still.

"Kissing doesn't count. I don't think, anyway."

She tried to chuckle at his teasing remark. He was trying hard to make this easy. Yet she felt as if she'd swallowed a lead weight. Pressing her palm against her stomach, she took another deep breath.

"You okay?" he asked.

"Sure."

After a moment he stood up. "Let's go into my office and get this over with."

Leaning over his desk, she touched the black ballpoint pen to the bottom of the official document to keep the shaking in her hand from showing. Her signature was not quite as neat as she would have liked, but it was her full legal name nonetheless.

The pen seemed to fairly fly across the page as Sean signed the papers that declared their short marriage null and void. As if it never happened.

"Done." He tossed the pen on the desk and straightened his back, sighing deeply.

"So I'm no longer Mrs. Sean Hudson."

His head cocked a fraction. "Funny, but I never really thought of you like that."

"Why should you?" But even as she grinned and gave a small lift of her shoulder in a show of light disregard, pain knifed straight through her heart, straight through her soul.

"Nicole Willis," he said cheerfully. "No, no. Not Nicole. Nicki. The world's best nanny. *That's* how I'll always think of you."

His words hurt her worse than a knife. They were like jagged claws, ripping and tearing at the most tender and vulnerable part of her.

Why? she wondered. Why should his words wound her? His breezy commentary shouldn't hurt her in the least. She had known all along that the flirtatious game they were playing was just that—a game. She had known he wasn't interested in an ongoing relationship. Neither was she. They had participated in the provocative amusement, both knowing that there would come a time when it all would end. That was the very reason she was able to act out this silly game. So why was she experiencing this awful torture hearing him verbalize only what she had already known to be true?

Because you love him.

No! Her silent denial was firm. That couldn't be true. She wouldn't allow it to be true.

Seconds ticked by. Awkwardness swelled and throbbed until she was positive it would burst and cover them both in some kind of harmful, viscous liquid that would surely burn them like acid. She needed to talk about something else, *anything* else, besides what their marriage had or hadn't been, or what the annulment meant, or how he'd forever remember her. She simply had to shut out any nuance of an idea that her affections for him were anything more than simple physical attraction—attraction she had been positive she could keep under tight control.

What she was feeling wasn't love. She struggled with the silent protestation, even though no other excuse lent itself as salvation. Loving Sean just wasn't a possibility. The chaos in her mind swirled and churned as she struggled for something to say.

"I—I wanted to tell you—" She heard the nervous, harried quality in her tone and stopped. After moistening her lips, she tried again. "I wanted to let you know..."

He turned to face her fully, and Nicki realized in that instant that there wasn't a more handsome man on the face of the earth. Oh, why had fate given him such gorgeous dark eyes?

His gaze was curious, probing as he waited in silence.

"I accepted a job," she exclaimed. "In Slovakia."

She had meant to ease into the subject. To tell him gently that she would be leaving soon. However, that was impossible now.

A frown etched deep into his forehead, and he was just about to respond when a fitful cry crackled over the baby monitor, alerting them that Sona had awakened.

His tone was soft as he said, "Excuse me a minute." And he slipped from the room.

Nicki picked up the documents and straightened them neatly by tapping them on the desktop. Then she slid them back into the large envelope. As the papers disappeared from view, Nicki felt overcome with a complete and utter desolation that was enough to make her eyes well with tears.

She would not cry. She would not! She was a grown woman. A mature adult. She had gotten involved in this whole scheme knowing the rules right up front. She couldn't expect them to change now.

"I don't want the rules to change," she

whispered the assertion. But even as she spoke, she knew what she said was a lie.

Well, she decided, she'd have to continue living the lie. Sean must never discover how she felt. He didn't think of her in that personal, profound, intimate way. Sure, he had flirted with her. Said sweet things. Teased her. Kissed her. But that had all been in fun. She knew it. And she knew *he* knew it. His lighthearted comments just now were proof of that. *"The world's greatest nanny,"* he'd called her. It was clear his affection for her ran no deeper than that.

That fact was what she must focus on during her remaining time here. That fact was what would make it possible for her to continue to hide her feelings from Sean for these few remaining days.

Hearing him sing, softly and lovingly, to his daughter, Nicki smiled to herself, despite the dark emotions shadowing over her. Sean loved Sona dearly. And the little girl had come to love her new daddy, too.

Sona kept saying one word over and over, and that word being relayed through the monitor had Nicki going into the kitchen. With her mind terribly preoccupied, she reached into the cabinet and pulled down a child's plastic sippey cup. She then went to the refrigerator for the bottle of apple juice and filled it.

Sean had reached the kitchen with Sona in his arms as Nicki was snapping on the lid.

"I'm sorry," Sean said to Nicki. "But I don't know what it is she's asking for. I thought I'd learned a lot of her language. But this is a new one to me."

"Dink," Sona said, looking imploringly at Nicki. "Dink."

"Here, honey." Nicki offered the toddler the cup of juice she'd prepared. Then she looked at Sean. "She wants a drink."

As soon as the last word left her mouth, Nicki gasped, her eyes going wide. She'd fixed the juice without consciously realizing what she'd heard over the intercom.

"She wants a *drink*," Nicki said.

Still, Sean didn't seem to understand the relevance.

"In *English*." Nicki was excited now. "She said it in English. She just dropped the R. Most children do at first. The sound of R is hard to master."

In an instant, Sean was as ecstatic about the event as she.

"My little girl's learning English!"

Sona giggled, her tired expression brightening. Nicki decided the child probably didn't understand why her daddy was so happy, but she seemed only too pleased to join in on the excitement.

"This calls for a celebration," Sean said.

Nicki went straight to the cabinet. "We need a toast. Apple juice all around?"

He laughed. "Apple juice would taste as good to me as champagne right now."

Glasses were filled and clinked together as Sean called out "To Sona!"

"To Sona!" Nicki parroted before taking a sip of cool juice. "You know, she'll be picking up words right and left, now. There will be no stopping her." Sean turned adoring eyes on his little girl. "This is great sweetheart. Soon daddy will be able to understand everything you say. And you'll understand me, too." His gaze glittered as he turned his attention to Nicki and asked, "Isn't this wonderful?"

She nodded, but in her heart she realized, in that one dreadful moment that the final piece of this complicated puzzle—her last remaining reason for staying here with Sean and Sona—had just snapped into place.

Their family picture was perfect. Complete. They didn't need her any longer.

After Sean had taken Sona back to her room, Nicki sat in one corner of the screened-in porch, oblivious to the chirping of the crickets, the high-pitched croaking of the tree frogs.

She hadn't been exaggerating when she'd told Sean that Sona would be unstoppable now. The child would pick up English words and phrases in no time at all. Children had a capacity to learn that was staggering. They were like dry sponges, sopping up, sucking in—almost to the point of inhaling—any information with which they were presented. Little Sona would be no different.

Within weeks, Nicki knew Sean's little girl would be spouting off nouns and verbs, and quickly learning to put together simple sentences. From there, communication between father and daughter would be unlimited.

Nicki also knew, beyond a shadow of a doubt, that when she left here, Sean and Sona would be just fine. However, she had to wonder about herself. Just how long would it take her to excavate this special man, and his precious daughter, from her heart?

Movement at the French doors had her lifting

her gaze. Sean stood, his hands planted on the door frame. The light behind him cast his face in darkness but emphasized his broad shoulders, his long, lean body. Nicki marveled at how the mere sight of him set her pulse to racing.

"Well," he said, "after three stories and a diaper change, she's finally settling in."

Nicki could only smile, hoping her desolation and sadness didn't show. The feelings were silly, anyway. But snuffing them out was impossible. The fact that he got Sona settled and into bed all by himself was just more evidence that his need of her had dwindled to a mere trickle, and that only made her misery worse.

"I think we need to talk," he said.

She nodded, knowing that even though the porch was dark, the light cast from the doorway illuminated her face enough so he could see her silent response. She simply didn't trust her voice enough yet to actually speak to him.

He came toward her, but stopped before he got too close. She was relieved when he didn't reach to snap on the overhead light. This discussion was better held in the shadows. Sean folded his arms tightly across the broad expanse of his chest, leaning his shoulder against one of the exposed, glossy-finished wall studs.

"How long have you known about the job?"

She felt the urge to retreat. But that would do no good. They had to have this conversation sometime. Now was as good a time as any.

"Not long," she said. "Only a couple of days."

His silence seemed to relay his disapproval.

"You knew I'd been inquiring." She moistened her suddenly dry lips. "That was the plan from the very beginning."

"You're right. I know."

There was defensiveness in his tone, and the last thing Nicki wanted was to argue with him. In fact, she was in no shape to spar. She was already too close to tears as it was. If his anger flared, or she became too distressed, she just might reveal more of her feelings than she should.

"I just wondered why you didn't tell me right away."

Because I didn't want to spoil all the fun we were having. Because I liked the way you flirted with me. The way you looked at me. The way you kissed me.

She couldn't tell him those things. So she said nothing.

He turned his head, focusing his gaze

somewhere out in the darkness of the backyard, and silence settled in for what threatened to be a long siege.

Minutes ticked by, and Nicki's agony only swelled and bulged, growing ever more uncomfortable. Their time together would soon be over. She had to deal with that. Get used to the idea. And move on.

So she'd made the mistake of falling in love with Sean. She'd get over it.

But even though she'd someday get over these intimate feelings for him, she would never stop caring about him. And even though he'd told her before that he was not interested in having a woman in his life, she still felt that would be the best thing for him.

She thought about Sona's visit to the pediatrician and how upset Sean had been. Once she left, he would have no one to lean on. He'd been terribly angry the last time she'd spoken her mind about his finding a wife. However, once she left she wouldn't have another opportunity to tell him he needed to open his heart to love.

Deciding then and there to chance stirring his ire, she wondered how best to go about bestowing what she knew would be unwanted advice.

"Sean," she said, and then she waited until he looked her way. "I'll be leaving soon."

He only had to turn his head a fraction of an inch to look at her. His broad chest rose and fell as he breathed.

"But," she continued, "I have something I'd like to say. Once I go away, I won't ever get a chance to tell you how I feel."

She'd piqued his interest, she could tell. His shoulders relaxed slightly and his head cocked a fraction as he locked his attention on her.

"Since coming here—" her mouth went dry, but she pushed forward "—I feel that we've... become friends."

Tension knotted his jaw muscle.

"I can't help but tell you again that... you need someone. You really do."

"Nicki—"

But she refused to let up. "Wait," she told him. "Please let me finish. I care about you. I care about Sona. I know I've made the arguments before, but I'll be worried about the two of you when I leave here. I just want you to tell me that you'll at least think about dating. That you'll at least try to imagine yourself with a woman who can... help you. Who can be a mommy to Sona."

She didn't want her thoughts to go into too much detail about what this other woman might do with Sean. What ecstasy this other woman might find in his arms. Simply knowing the man she loved wasn't alone would be enough. It would have to be.

"Promise me that, once I'm gone," she tried again, "you'll work on finding yourself a wife."

He sighed. His arms falling to his sides as he came toward her.

"Oh, Nicki." He sat down next to her. "It makes me feel good to know you care. About me. About Sona."

She didn't know what to say. She'd steeled herself for his anger. This calm emphatic response wasn't what she'd expected, so she hadn't a clue what to say.

"You're right," he said. "We *have* become friends. And I know I owe you so much. I want you to understand. I want you to let me explain—" he hesitated long enough to take her hand in his "—why I can never make that promise to you."

Chapter Ten

"She was so young."

His voice flowed over Nicki like heated velvet, caressing and whisper soft, but an underlying tension in his words put her on edge... a disconcerting combination.

"Only nineteen." A taut sigh issued from between his lips. "I loved her." He quickly stressed, "I *did*." He gazed over her shoulder into the night as he spoke, and Nicki couldn't help but wonder if he'd emphasized the point for her sake—or his own.

He shook his head, his tone growing faint as he added, "But we were just too young to get married." Nicki sat, silent and pensive. His relationship with this young woman must have been serious if thoughts of marriage were linked to the memory.

"She'd graduated high school the year before," he continued. "She had a full-time job. She was ready to start the next phase of her life, which was, in her mind, marriage, children, a home... a happily-ever-after surrounded by a lush, green lawn and a white picket fence." He absently rubbed his fingers back and forth across his jaw. "Me? I was just entering my third year of college. Barely twenty. Nowhere near making that kind of commitment or taking on the responsibilities of a wife and family. I had too many ambitions where my education was concerned.

"She spoke of our wedding often," he said. "I tried to be patient. Tried to explain my goals in a way that wouldn't hurt her feelings. But she just didn't seem to understand."

Nicki felt his deep, intense gaze on her face, but she doubted that he even saw her. He was in another place. Another time.

"Maybe she understood," he whispered, "but she was intent on achieving her own goals." He exhaled forcefully. "I don't know."

He leaned away from her, resting his elbows on his knees. His neck muscles relaxed slightly so that his head hung slightly downward. He stared at his clasped hands, or the floor, Nicki couldn't tell which since his position now hid his face from her view. He heaved a deep sigh. A sigh that told her something was coming. Something big. Something bad. And whatever it was, Sean dreaded the telling, that much was clearly evident. Nicki's breath caught and held as she waited for him to share what must surely be an awful memory.

"She came to my dorm room one day," he said, his voice grating with suppressed emotion. "She pushed me about setting a date. Again. I kept telling her that the time wasn't right. I didn't want to hurt her. I never meant to hurt her. But she pushed and pushed. And then she blurted out that she wanted to get married right then. Right at the start of my junior year. I told her it was a ridiculous idea. That we had to wait. She acted like she didn't even hear me. She'd work, she said. While I went to school. Our lives would be perfect, she said."

His inhalation was ragged. "I boiled over. Completely lost control. I was so frustrated and angry. Didn't she understand what I was trying to do? I asked her. I was working toward a *degree*. Didn't that *mean* anything to her? I said so many things, I don't even remember all of them now. But what I do remember was turning her down. Unequivocally. I told her I wasn't getting married—to her or anyone else—for a very long time. *Not for years.*" He rubbed his hands over his face. "She called me names. Ranted and raved. Then she ran out, sobbing so loudly that people had begun to poke their heads out of their doors to see what all the commotion was about."

Sean went utterly still, and Nicki had to force herself not to touch him. Not yet. Something in her told her now wasn't the time. He was too wrapped up in events of the past.

"She drove off—" his voice caught, but he swallowed and then finished "—and promptly caused a five-car accident on the highway."

Nicki was afraid her horrified gasp would disturb him. However, he was too caught up in his memory to even be aware of her reaction.

"By the time I got to the hospital," he said, "it was too late."

"Oh, Sean—" This time, the impulse to reach out to him was too great to deny. She slid her hand over his biceps. "She died?"

"No."

The single word seemed to be wrenched from

him, and Nicki frowned in confusion. Then what had he meant by...

"But our baby did." His huge sigh was filled with an all-consuming misery. "She miscarried. And I hadn't even known she'd been pregnant."

He seemed to isolate himself, his emotions, from the present. And Nicki knew that nothing she could say would comfort him at this moment. She pulled her hand away from his arm, pressing it flat against her chest, against her heart that ached so for him.

"I was so damned selfish," he vented angrily. "I was so wrapped up in what *I* wanted, in what *I* intended to have, that I refused to listen to her. I didn't hear what she was saying—what she was trying to relay—in those pleadings for marriage. She was in trouble. She was pregnant with my child. She was scared. And I turned her down. I turned her away."

He raked his fingers through his hair. "My callousness, my domineering nature, my stubbornness... but most of all my self-centeredness caused the death of my own child."

A single breath tore from his chest, and Nicki was certain he was going to break down. But he held firm, releasing the exhalation with teetering restraint.

Nicki wanted desperately to hold him, but not knowing how he'd react, she kept her hands to herself.

"I vowed back then," he continued softly, "that I wouldn't inflict pain on another woman. I wouldn't let anyone fall in love with me. I wouldn't allow anyone to get close enough to get hurt. I'm just not fit to be a partner. That was clear to me then. Just as it's clear to me now."

In that moment, Nicki understood. When she'd first met Sean, she had suspected he didn't want to become involved because he'd been hurt by a woman. But now she knew the truth. Sean refused to become involved because *he was the one who had done the hurting*.

The idea that he would forgo happiness, that he would deny himself the love and companionship, the sharing and tenderness that a life partner would bring was overwhelmingly heart-wrenching for Nicki. Tears welled in her eyes, inflicting pinpricks of pain as emotion filled her heart, her chest, her whole body. She felt for him. Sadness and regret for what he obviously saw as his callous actions toward the young woman, and the unbearable grief he suffered—then and even now—for his beloved child... the child of whom he'd been unaware until it was too late.

Then Nicki was struck with a realization. Sean had made some pretty tough life decisions for himself because he felt guilty about events that had taken place in the past—*events over which he'd had little or no control.*

"Sean," she said in the stillness.

He didn't respond, didn't move a muscle, and she decided that he was still lost in his horrible memories. The urge to rescue him washed over her, engulfed her like rising, swirling floodwaters, and at that moment, all she wanted to do was help him break free of the past.

Sliding her hand over his shoulder, she gave a gentle tug. "Sean, listen to me."

He turned toward her, and the look on his face nearly ripped her heart in two. His eyes had lost their intensity, even in the dim light of the porch she could see it. He seemed lethargic, as if he'd been running a long, endless race for ages and he was just plain tired.

"You can't blame yourself," she said. "You didn't know she was pregnant. You didn't know about the baby when she drove off."

"I can blame myself," he told her.

There wasn't anger in his tone. Only candid honesty.

"And I do." He paused long enough to swallow. "If I hadn't been so domineering, Christine would have felt comfortable enough to tell me the truth. I rejected her, and she blindly ran away and got involved in an accident that took our baby's life. I'll always feel responsible. Always."

Surprisingly, Nicki understood. She smoothed her fingers up his forearm and then back down, trying in vain to give him some small measure of comfort.

"You know," she began, "we're often told to put the past behind us. To learn from our mistakes and try hard not to repeat them. To forget the past and move on. But I believe that life has handed you a situation that can't be forgotten. It can't even be transcended." She curled her fingers around his wrist. "It simply has to be lived with."

He actually seemed relieved when he realized she wasn't going to try to talk him out of feeling guilty about the events of long ago.

"I also believe," she continued, "that the person you have become is a direct result of what you have experienced in your past. I believe that's true of everyone. You. Me." She cocked her head slightly to one side. "Everyone."

She softened her tone as she added, "If you hadn't rejected Christine, if you hadn't turned away from your first opportunity to have a family, then ...who knows? You might never have felt the urge to respond to Sona's desperate need for a parent, for a home, when you saw that television program. And I'll tell you something else ...you may feel badly about what you see as your self-seeking behavior in the past, but taking that little girl in when she had nothing and nowhere to go is the most unselfish act there is."

Nicki could see from the light sparking in his eyes that she was forcing him to think. It was a small fight—a tiny ray of hope, Nicki mused—but it was there nonetheless. For the first time it seemed, he was pondering his situation, his past, from a different angle.

"I'm not about to tell you to forget the past," she said. "But I am going to tell you it's time to forgive. And the person you need to forgive is yourself." With each statement she made, his spine became a little straighter. His brow furrowed a little deeper. He was considering all she had to say with intense concentration.

"We can't change the past." She let her hand slide down over his fingers and she gave them a gentle squeeze. "We can only do our best to make a satisfying future for ourselves and the people we love." Pulling her hand away from him, she slid to the very edge of the seat. She wanted to be as close to him as possible when she expressed her final words.

"I've come to care a great deal about you and Sona," she told him. "You might be angry about what I'm going to say, but what you just told me hasn't changed my mind. I still feel you need a woman in your life."

Before he could respond, she rushed on. "When I think about the scary moments you've had with Sona, like when she tumbled out of her crib... or the worrisome times, like when you took her to the doctor... and even the wonderful moments, like tonight when she spoke her first word of English, it makes me very sad to think that, once I leave here, you won't have anyone you can share those things with."

Meaning to emphasize her point, she pressed her cupped palm over his knee and said, "You *need* to find someone. You *deserve* to have someone."

He looked her full in the face, and she steeled herself for his anger.

But it didn't come.

The seconds ticked by seemingly in slow motion. The expression on his face was unreadable. Was that indecision she saw in his dark gaze? Then she watched as his tongue glided out to moisten his lips. His jaw tightened in what looked to be sudden resolve.

Then he blurted out, "I don't want just anyone— *I want you.*"

***

Why the hell hadn't he held his tongue? Why had he let those words come spewing from his mouth?

Because he'd had no control over them, that's why. In that one moment of weakness, he'd allowed his emotions to reveal themselves. And now he'd frightened Nicki away forever.

And frightened was exactly what she'd been when she fled from the porch.

First, she'd looked startled. Then, in a flash, fear had etched into every angle of her beautiful face. Her skin had suddenly stretched taut over her cheekbones. Her eyes had widened with what he could only describe as sheer and utter dread. Even her nostrils had flared with the fear he'd invoked in her.

And then she'd bolted.

If he'd only kept his mouth shut, he wouldn't be sitting here. All alone. In the dark.

While explaining the death of his child to Nicki, he'd been plagued by emotions so dismal and daunting that he thought he just might fall into the huge bottomless pit of his memory, lost forever in the horror of it all. Like some sort of miracle worker, Nicki had tugged and pulled at him with her soft, comforting words until she'd dragged him free, back into the here and now.

What she'd said had made sense. Some events that happen can't ever be forgotten... he never intended to forget his child. And some actions and behaviors, no matter how regretful they were, couldn't be risen above, either. As Nicki said, these memories simply had to be lived with.

She had been correct, too, he decided, when she'd proclaimed that people are molded by their past. He was proud of the fact that Nicki thought his adopting Sona was an unselfish act. He hadn't thought of it in that manner before. Maybe his past experiences *had* helped to shape him into a better person.

"*The person you have become,*" her exact words echoed through his mind, "*is a direct result of what you have experienced in your past.*"

As he worried over his current situation with Nicki, he couldn't help but feel that what she'd said was an important key to unlocking, not only the mysteries of who he was and what he had endured, but her own plight as well.

That fear that had overwhelmed her just a moment ago niggled at him. Her behavior puzzled him. It disturbed him, too. No one should have to suffer being so afraid. But what was it that had her so scared? What continued to trigger that deeply ingrained panic in her?

He'd seen it before, he remembered. When he'd first kissed her in the upstairs hallway all those weeks ago. He'd kissed her, and she had run from him like a panic-stricken doe. And the next day she'd threatened to leave. Only his plea of needing her had changed her mind about abandoning him and Sona there and then.

His thoughts raced. He'd come to the initial conclusion back then that she was afraid of intimacy... that her inexperience with men had her feeling skittish. But he'd soon learned that wasn't so. After the bubble bath incident—Sean grinned at the memory, despite the chaos churning in him—they had begun flirting. It had been fun and frivolous... and Nicki had seemed to enjoy herself just as much as he had.

Maybe she'd been able to relax because what had taken place between them *had* been fun and frivolous, with *frivolous* being the operative word. Light-hearted. Meaningless. As long as the flirtatiousness remained on the superficial level, she felt safe. Was that it? He frowned. Could it be that, as long as their attraction had been some sort of amusing sport, then she was willing to play?

Their relationship would never turn serious... at least that's what their trivial game had implied. It's what they both had mistakenly thought. What they both had verbalized. Their attraction was physical, easily cast aside when it was time for her to go. That's why she'd felt safe to participate.

But why was she so intent on leaving?

The lure they felt for one another—the powerful electricity—was mutual, anyone could have figured that out. And Nicki certainly wasn't a shallow person. She was kind and caring and extremely concerned about those around her. This whole situation seemed like such a contradiction. It didn't make sense.

Frustration had him grinding his teeth. He felt as if he had lots of bits and scraps of information regarding who Nicki was, what she felt, and why, but the pieces just didn't seem to fit into any kind of coherent picture.

A person is molded by the past.

The concept flitted through his mind again. Could this fear Nicki felt be provoked by something from her past?

She'd been abandoned by a mother who hadn't wanted her. Passed from foster home to foster home.

She'd gone into teaching because the children needed her. She'd left the United States... Why? Sean wondered. She'd left the country after she'd graduated from college and she hadn't returned, as far as he was aware, until she'd agreed to help with Sona.

Did all of America represent a place where she wasn't wanted?

Two words seemed to keep popping up again and again: *want* and *need.*

Nicki hadn't felt wanted as a child. And every time he'd intimated, through physical acts or words, that he wanted her or desired her, she would panic.

She taught English to foreign children who needed her. And he'd been able to talk her into helping him, persuade her to stay when she'd threatened to leave, time and again, by explaining how much he needed her.

She needed to be needed. That was easy enough to work out.

But she feared being wanted.

The revelation had him worrying his chin between his index finger and thumb.

Could she somehow have reasoned that being wanted left her vulnerable to the whims and emotions of others? Left her vulnerable to being hurt?

He got up, paced to the doorway that led into the house. There he stood, listening to the quiet.

At that moment Sean felt he understood Nicki a little better. The motives that drove her, that made her think the way she did. That made her care so deeply, that made her yearn to be needed. That made her afraid of the fact that he wanted her.

Now he felt that the task of a lifetime was set before him. And that formidable undertaking would be to make Nicki understand herself, understand the awesome fear that plagued her... before she got on a airplane and flew out of his life forever.

***

She was leaving.

With an odd mixture of sadness, regret, and apprehension, Nicki tucked the plain cotton blouse into her suitcase, closed the lid and snapped shut the latch. Lifting the duffle bag up off the mattress, she set it on the floor and then automatically reached to smooth out the wrinkles in the bedspread.

She had no idea what had happened to her over the past twenty-four hours. All she knew was that she had to leave. Immediately.

Last night on the porch after Sean had told her he wanted her, Nicki had been consumed by a dread so dark and terrible that she felt it was a monster that threatened to swallow her whole, a monster from which there was no escape.

She loved Sean. She knew that. And hearing him say that he wanted her *should* have made her deliriously happy. So why hadn't it?

Instead, she'd suddenly felt like a little girl. A

defenseless child sitting in a pitch-black room, fearing the mean and ugly bogeyman, knowing he was coming for her at any moment.

The feeling had been more than she could handle, so she had done the only thing she could: she'd run. She fled to save herself. It had been an instinctive act. A natural reflex she couldn't have squelched, even if she'd wanted to.

She'd burrowed under her covers all night, feeling sure that something awful was going to happen. And she awoke this morning with the same terrible dread weighing heavily in her stomach. So she decided she had to get out. She *had* to go. And her teaching assignment in Slovakia was the perfect escape.

Sean had accepted the news this morning very well, considering the way she had left him so abruptly last night. He hadn't asked any questions, only told her he would do what he could to get her a transatlantic flight for tomorrow. She'd successfully avoided him for the rest of the day. So she had her meager possessions packed in anticipation of the trip to the airport in the morning.

She'd miss little Sona. Nicki's lips curled at the corners when she imagined the child's innocent little face, her blunt-cropped hair that was now shiny from the healthy diet her new daddy was providing, her dark eyes that grew so large with curiosity, her quick smile and bubbly laughter. Sona was a beautiful little girl, and Nicki knew the child would bloom like a lovely flower under Sean's loving care.

Sean... she'd miss him, too. He was a man who—

Ice seemed to freeze in her veins. Apprehension so awful that she felt she couldn't breathe. Her heart pounded. Perspiration prickled her brow.

"Stop." She pressed her palm flat against the base of her throat, inhaling with difficulty, slow and deep, as she tried to ease the panic that swept through her.

She had to get thoughts of Sean out of her mind. Now. She moved toward the door and opened it. The glow of the moonlight filtering in through the bathroom window dimly lit the hallway. Nicki stopped outside Sona's door. She heard the toddler playing inside. She'd spend some time with the child.

Say goodbye. Nicki needed something to engage her thoughts, to help her overcome this terrible torment churning in the pit of her belly.

Pushing open the door, Nicki had to grin at Sona

and Sean at play on the carpet. The toddler was trying to balance a block on top of her daddy's head. Sean sat on the floor, patiently holding himself still, and Sona giggled with glee each time the colorful block toppled to the floor.

"Hi," Nicki called to them softly.

The little girl said, "Hi," right back with no hesitation, and Nicki was once again reminded of the incredible learning ability of children.

Sean swooped Sona onto his lap. "Aren't you just the smartest little girl in the universe?" he asked, then he nibbled his daughter's ear as she bubbled with laughter. Then he looked at Nicki. "Come in."

Nicki entered, feeling tentative. "I just thought I'd spend a little time with Sona... before, you know."

His head bobbed, but he said nothing.

Sona scrambled from her daddy's embrace and toddled over to Nicki, taking her hand. Then the little girl led her to where Sean was sitting and pulled Nicki down to sit beside him. Handing Nicki a wooden block, Sona made it clear that she wanted Nicki to join in the game of balancing a block atop Sean's head.

Biting her bottom lip, Nicki stared at the block,

focusing on its glossy, sky-blue color. The corner of the wood block bit into Nicki's thumb as she bided her time, putting off the inevitable. She'd come in here to be with Sona, but there would be no interacting with the child without associating with Sean. In the back of her mind, she had to have known that.

Stirring her resolve, she lifted her chin... and her gaze collided with the most intense stare she'd ever encountered in her life.

There were messages being relayed in his deep mahogany eyes. Messages she simply wasn't prepared to decipher. Not now. Not when she was already engaged in battling this fearful chaos inside her.

Sona's frustration became apparent.

Letting her gaze slide from his, Nicki looked up and focused on placing the block gently on his silky, nut-brown hair.

The toddler clapped and laughed. Nicki and Sean couldn't help but smile at her unfettered glee. It took so little to delight her. Nicki felt a tremendous satisfaction in having a small hand in Sona's secure and happy future.

Movement out of the corner of her eye had Nicki

starting out of her moment of reverie. Instinctively, she jerked to reach for the block as it fell.

Sean reacted to the very same reflex.

The block plopped in Nicki's palm, Sean's warm hand cupping hers.

Their gazes met. And held. Although he didn't move a muscle, Nicki felt as though she were being stroked... caressed. Her exhalation was shaky.

Evidently bored with these tedious adults, Sona swiped the block from Nicki's hand and toddled toward her toy box.

Slowly, slowly, Nicki pulled her hand from where it rested in Sean's. She averted her gaze to the floor.

He captured her chin between his gentle fingers and applied just enough pressure to have her looking at his face.

"Please, Nicki..."

His voice was as soft as the wings of a lazy luna moth.

"Talk to me," He pleaded. His voice swelled with deep emotion as he added, "Trust me.

Fear gripped her with icy claws. All the air seemed to rush from her lungs in a loud whoosh, but Nicki knew the sound, the feeling, were all in her imagination. Still, the fright pumping through her was intimidating and unrelenting.

She had no idea why Sean triggered this feeling in her, she only knew she felt it. Fully. Completely. In every fiber of her being. It took every nuance of control to remain seated here beside him.

"Nicki."

The entreaty she heard in his tone only seemed to increase the anxiety churning in her chest.

He was so good, so kind. He'd become her friend over the past few weeks. Why did he provoke this awful feeling in her?

She swallowed, her throat dry, rough, grating as desert sand. "I'm scared."

"I know, honey," he said. "I know you are." His tone died to a mere whisper. "I'd like you to tell me about it."

Again, she experienced that sense of being in a vacuum, of having no air to breathe.

"I—I'm just," she stammered, "scared."

Evidently, he realized she couldn't expound further.

"As long as our relationship remained breezy," he said, "with that false kind of flirting fun, you were okay. But the moment things turned the least bit serious... the instant we seemed to connect, your eyes would fill with sheer terror."

She nodded slowly. "That's true. It's what I'm feeling now."

He empathized with her agony, it showed in his gorgeous, dark eyes.

His compassion seemed to bolster her, and she found the strength to fight back the fear. Her tone trembled as she said, "I feel like a little kid. Waiting. And watching. It's all so... strange. So... infantile. Yet, it's more real than anything I've ever experienced. It's like I *know* something is surely going to come and... and..." She felt so silly finally admitting, "Get me."

Disgust at her weakness filled her and she looked away.

"Honey—"

The gentleness in that one little word was enough to melt her heart right in her chest.

"—could it be," he continued, "that you're not afraid that something is going to come, but that someone *isn't* going to come?"

She frowned, confused. What could he mean?

"All those years you were in those foster homes," he explained, taking her hand in his, "you waited for someone. Someone to adopt you. Someone to love you. Someone to *want* you."

The panic inside her flared red-hot. Sudden tears seared her eye sockets. She was bombarded by the overwhelming urge to escape him... no, not him... but the memories—*the truth*—he was speaking.

His warm palm and fingers curled protectively around her hand and acted as a lanyard to sanity, to strength. His words stirred her fear, yes, but she desperately wanted to move beyond this dread, escape it, banish it forever. Somehow, she instinctively knew Sean meant to help her do just that.

"And when they didn't come," he continued, "you shut yourself off. You decided to protect yourself. From pain and hurt. By refusing to be loved. By refusing to be wanted."

Her frown deepened. Could this terror she'd been experiencing really be traced back to something so simple? she wondered.

He was right about their flirting. There had been times when she'd reveled in it. She guessed that was because she had expected the playfulness to be quite forgettable. Oh, but how quickly she'd realized that idea was nothing but dead wrong.

She'd fallen in love with Sean. Fallen into a deep chasm of emotion from which there was no escape. And that's when the panic and fear in her really rose to such unbearable heights.

"I want you, Nicki," he said. "I love you. And even if you run away from me, what I'm feeling for you isn't going to change."

She was amazed that on the outside she seemed so calm, when on the inside she was a mass of chaotic hysteria. *The monster is coming*, a puerile voice in her mind kept chanting. *It's going to get you. Run. Run!*

But the love she felt for Sean was like a tiny beacon in the ebony blackness of her thoughts. It was almost as if he'd opened that imaginary door that the little girl in her feared, and the grisly and empty space behind it, the place that so terrified her wasn't empty. Sean filled that doorway... with his hand outstretched to her.

He squeezed her hand with gentle pressure. "You helped me understand that I was meant to learn from my past mistakes... not atone for them forever. Before you came into my life, I was half a person. I could be wrong, but I have a feeling that maybe you've felt the same way." His voice softened as he suggested, "Maybe, just maybe, together, we can be whole."

Oh, Lord, how she wanted to feel complete. She wanted to be loved. To know love. To give love. Oh, how she wanted to be wanted!

The lump in her throat made it nearly impossible to speak, but she was determined to tell him how she felt.

"Sean—" his name came out sounding as scratchy as steel wool "—I love you."

He tugged her onto his lap and she snuggled her face into the crook of his neck. He smelled good. Like warm citrus. Like security. Like love.

"I love you, too," he whispered against her hair. "More than words can express."

Pushing against his chest, she looked at him, wide-eyed. "But what about the plane ticket for tomorrow?"

His face screwed into a sheepish expression.

"There is no plane ticket for tomorrow." He smoothed his index finger down the length of her jawbone. "I was determined to tell you how I felt. I was determined to make you decide to stay here with me and Sona. So determined... that I tore up the annulment papers."

Her jaw dropped; her lips parting.

"You—you destroyed the papers?"

He nodded.

Nicki couldn't believe it. She was still Sean's wife.

I was determined.... His words rang like joyous bells in her head.

He'd shown that same kind of resolve in adopting Sona, even to the point of marrying Nicki on the spot to make his plans happen. Sean was a very determined man.

Grinning up at him, she injected as much sultry sexiness into her voice as she could muster as she said, "Determination is one of your greatest assets."

She kissed him, full on the mouth. A kiss that proved beyond a shadow of a doubt how she felt.

"I am determined," he whispered huskily against her lips, "to give you a safe haven. A loving home. A happily-ever-after. I'm also determined to give you a real wedding. One you'll never forget. You, of all people, sure deserve it."

Knowing Sona played contentedly behind them, Nicki relished Sean's strong arms pulling her tightly against him. They kissed, and Nicki knew this was the beginning of a bright future for them all.

Epilogue

"**I**, Sean, take you, Nicole..."

In total awe, Nicki studied the handsome face of the man she loved.

"To be my wedded wife."

The white lace of her gown made her feel like a princess. The love shining in Sean's eyes made her feel like a queen.

"To have and to hold, from this day forward..." She thought to look down at little Sona, who she knew stood between the two of them, pretty as a priceless painting in her pink satin dress; however, Nicki was mesmerized by the intense darkness of Sean's eyes. She felt lost in them—no, she felt *found by them!*

Before Nicki realized it, she was prompted by the

reverend to repeat the wedding vows... words that would tie her to Sean for the rest of their lives. Excitement danced in her heart, but she had no problem speaking. Loudly. Clearly.

After they exchanged rings, the minister said, "By the power vested in me by the Commonwealth of Pennsylvania, I now pronounce you man and wife. You may kiss the bride."

The kiss was firm and warm and filled with loving promise.

Bob Davis, Sean's caretaker, and Bob's wife, Joan, congratulated the newlyweds, having happily and eagerly agreed to stand up for the couple.

Sean then reached down and picked up Sona. "Hey, there, sweet pea," he said, kissing the child on her silky cheek. The toddler grinned at her new mommy and then hugged her daddy around the neck.

Clasping hands, the little family started down the aisle of the church. Their happily ever after had begun.

*****

Thank you for taking the time to read A Beautiful Stranger. If you enjoyed the book, please tell a friend about it or consider writing a review.

Word-of-mouth recommendation is the best advertising tool an author can have!

A Note From the Author

I love it when two people come together for the sake of a vulnerable child and they end up falling madly in love. I have used the theme in other books and I've tied them all together in a sweet romance series called A Family Forever. I hope you'll look for other books in the series.

Let's keep in touch. Please consider joining my mailing list so you will be alerted to New Releases, sale promotions, favorite recipes, giveaways, and more. I will never share your email address!

All my love,
Donna Fasano

FOLLOWING HIS HEART, Ocean City Boardwalk Series, Book 1

Sara Carson is a 30-something widow with a busy life. Two fun-loving best friends, a caring mom who needs her, and a thriving sweet shop. What more could a woman want? But when the ancient plumbing in her shop springs a leak and a gorgeous, dark-eyed stranger rushes to her rescue, hilarity unfolds—and Sara quickly sees exactly what she's been missing.

Something most peculiar draws Landon Richards to Ocean City, Maryland—and to the lovely Sara. This woman touches his heart like no other, and the two of them explore the heady attraction that pulses between them. But haunting dreams have a way of encroaching on reality, and the strange phenomenon that brings these two together will also threaten to tear them apart.

Available in paperback and for Kindle, Nook, iBooks, Kobo, and Google Play.

TWO HEARTS IN WINTER, Ocean City Boardwalk Series, Book 2

Loss and betrayal have caused Heather Phillips to give up on love. She's thrown herself into running The Lonely Loon, her Bed and Breakfast located on the boardwalk of Ocean City, Maryland. The "off season" in this tourist town is usually a time of rest and reflection for her; however, DB Atwell, a famous author, arrives at The Loon for the winter to finish his long-overdue novel. Daniel, too, has faced grief, and tragedy continues to haunt him. Once Heather and Daniel meet, their lives will never be the same.

Reminiscent of Nights in Rodanthe by Nicholas Sparks and culminating in a happily-ever-after similar to the great Nora Roberts, Two Hearts in

TWO HEARTS IN WINTER, Ocean City Boardwalk Series, Book 2

Winter is a story about learning to let go of the past, about realizing that, though hardship affects us, it need not define us, and about coming to understand and truly believe that beauty is sometimes covered in scars. The human heart has an amazing ability to forgive, to heal, and to hope, especially when touched by love.

Available in paperback and for Kindle, Nook, iBooks, Kobo, and Google Play.

WILD HEARTS OF SUMMER, Ocean City Boardwalk Series, Book 3

Cathy Whitley's two best friends, Sara and Heather, may have found the men of their dreams... and that's all well and good for them. But that's not going to happen to Cathy. She allowed love to catch her off-guard once and it drained her dry, emotionally and financially. She'll never let it happen again. Ever.

Brad Henderson has been chasing Cathy for years. He's settled for their on-again-off-again, "friends with bennies" relationship for far longer than he expected. Attempting to scale the stone wall she's built around her heart has left him scraped and bruised. When he inherits a business worth millions, he is sure she'll see him in a new light. Right?

One way or the other, it's time to draw a line in the sand...

Available February 2017 in paperback and for Kindle, Nook, iBooks, Kobo, and Google Play.

AN ALMOST PERFECT CHRISTMAS, Ocean City Boardwalk Series, Book 4

When it comes to business, Aaron Chase knows how to succeed. But when his daughter, Izzie, asks him for the perfect family Christmas, the handsome widower feels at a loss about how to make his little girl's dream come true.

Pediatric Nurse Christy Cooper has dedicated her life to taking care of children. She agrees to act as Izzie's stand-in mom for this special holiday and throws herself into making the child's Christmas wish a reality. Maybe this selfless act will somehow alleviate her secret regrets and failures of the past.

The holiday is filled with fun and laughter, and it's amazing how three short days can be so life-changing. When the impish eight-year-old talks the adults into acting out a silly, make-believe wedding, young Izzie is certain the magic of the season will turn the pretend vows into the real thing. The little girl wants her daddy to have Christmas in his life—every single day.

Available in paperback and for Kindle, Nook, iBooks, Kobo, and Google Play.

GROWN UP CHRISTMAS LIST, Ocean City Boardwalk Series, Book 5

Dina Griffin flees a dangerous situation and ends up in Ocean City, Maryland where she hopes to spend the holidays in hiding. Trusting no one, she wants only one thing this Christmas—to feel safe. Then Officer Gav Thomas threatens to arrest her for shoplifting. *Shoplifting?*

Gav is certain there's something Dina isn't telling him about her visit to his seaside town, so he devises a means to stick close to the vulnerable beauty. An unexpected attraction sparks, fierce enough to heat up the salt-tinged, wintry nights.

But the trouble Dina had hoped to escape arrives at her doorstep, bringing with it stark-raving fear and the realization that she *must* place her trust in someone.

Is Gav really just a local cop... or is he Dina's guardian angel?

Available now in paperback and for Kindle, Nook, iBooks, Kobo, and Google Play.

THE WEDDING PLANNER'S SON, Ocean City Boardwalk Series, Book 6

Tawny is a driven, high-achiever who fully expects to someday run the family business. But when her corporate exec parents attempt to use her as a pawn, Tawny flees to the only place she's ever felt happy—the beach.

Jack Barclay spends his summer days creating romantic seaside weddings for lovers. His laid-back attitude has served him well over the years. Stressing out about work only causes a person to miss the best parts of life.

Jack and Tawny are as different as sea and sky, but the fascination they find in each others company can't be denied. So they embark on a temporary, no-strings-attached romance with eyes wide open. What could possibly go wrong?

Coming, Spring 2017, in paperback and for Kindle, Nook, iBooks, Kobo, and Google Play.

Other Books by Donna Fasano

Other Books by Donna Fasano

The Single Daddy Club Series: Jason, Book 2
The Single Daddy Club Series: Reece, Book 3
Take Me, I'm Yours
His Wife for a While
An Accidental Family
Mountain Laurel
A Beautiful Stranger, A Family Forever, Book 1
and others

Non-fiction Books
Cooking In All Directions
Prayer of Quiet
Favorite Christmas Cookies
Recipes of Love
Guy Food

About The Author

Donna Fasano is a USA TODAY Bestselling
Author whose books have sold nearly 4 million
copies worldwide and have been translated into
two dozen languages. She lives on Maryland's
Eastern Shore with her husband and Roo, their
twelve-year-old Australian cattle dog mix.

www.ingramcontent.com/pod-product-compliance
Lightning Source LLC
Chambersburg PA
CBHW050025180626
46810CB00002B/575